'I think you're going to be something of a challenge, Dr Barrymore,' Jonathan said quietly. 'But I'm prepared to take a chance.'

How magnanimous! Lucinda stood up, her blue eyes levelling with his as he lounged against the desk. She would have liked to tell him to go to hell, but she wanted the job. It was a perfect opportunity for her to gain first-class experience in obstetrics, and to implement her own ideas on the subject. Not to mention the burning personal question that had haunted her ever since she'd discovered that this was the hospital where she'd been born to a mother she had never seen.

She gave him a saccharine smile as she swallowed her pride. 'I'm glad you're prepared to take a chance. When would you like me to start?'

'You can settle yourself in this morning and start work this afternoon.'

He pulled himself to his full height, towering above her. 'I hope you've got lots of stamina, Dr Barrymore, because I can be an absolute slave-driver. To be honest, when I first saw you just now, my heart sank. You look much too fragile for the job. I shall expect you to prove me wrong.'

Margaret Barker pursued a variety of interesting careers before she became a full-time author. Besides holding a BA degree in French and Linguistics she is a Licentiate of the Royal Academy of Music, a State Registered Nurse and a qualified teacher. While living in Africa Margaret had a radio programme with the Nigerian Broadcasting Corporation. Happily married for more than thirty years, she has two sons, a daughter and an increasing number of grandchildren. Her travels in Europe, Asia, Africa and America have given Margaret the background for her foreign novels and her own teaching hospital in England has provided ideas for her Medical Romances. She lives with her husband in a sixteenth-century thatched house near the sea.

Previous Titles

FORGIVE AND FORGET
BEDSIDE MANNERS
SURGEON RIVALS
ISLAND HONEYMOON

LOVING CARE

BY

MARGARET BARKER

MILLS & BOON LIMITED
ETON HOUSE 18–24 PARADISE ROAD
RICHMOND SURREY TW9 1SR

First published in Great Britain 1991
by Mills & Boon Limited

This edition 1991

ISBN 0 263 77218 7

Set in 10½ on 12 pt Linotron Times
03-9104-47164
Typeset in Great Britain by Centracet, Cambridge
Made and printed in Great Britain

CHAPTER ONE

So THIS was the famous Dr Jonathan Rathbone! Lucinda experienced a tremor of excitement running through her as the tall, dark figure approached. The palm of her hand felt sweaty as she extended it towards him. He grasped it firmly in his own and she wondered if he would notice her nervousness. She'd waited a long time for this confrontation and she was going to make the most of it!

No, that was unfair, she thought, as she looked up into the dark brown eyes. She must try not to think of their meeting as a confrontation. After all, he was now her boss, so she'd better toe the line—initially, that was! After the honeymoon period of her new employment she was going to show him her true colours! And she was going to make life difficult for him if he tried any of his high-handed tactics with her. It had been bad enough liaising with the great Dr Rathbone from St Celine's Hospital, but working with him was going to tax her patience to the full.

'We meet at last, Dr Barrymore,' Jonathan Rathbone said as he relinquished her hand.

Lucinda had an almost irrespressible urge to giggle. He sounded so formal! Most people called her Lucinda, but maybe it was better to keep their relationship as professional as possible. Because when she started making the changes she planned it would make things easier.

'We do indeed, Dr Rathbone,' she replied evenly. 'After all our telephone conversations regarding the patients I transferred to you I feel I've known you a long time.'

He smiled, and Lucinda noticed, for the first time, that he was quite good-looking. No, if she was honest with herself, he was positively handsome in a rugged sort of way. He was younger than she'd imagined; he couldn't be more than thirty-eight or thirty-nine. And the black hair wasn't slicked back in the severe style she'd visualised as she'd wrangled with him over the phone. Although she could see a trace of the grey hairs she had attributed to him, for he had the odd silver streak that only added to his attractiveness.

'Do sit down.' He motioned towards the chair in front of his desk as he moved behind and eased himself into the large leather swivel seat.

She watched him warily as he put the tips of his long, slender fingers together, his eyes narrowing when he studied her across the desk. She wondered if he'd deliberately kept her waiting for half an hour in his consulting-room.

'I must admit I was surprised when I heard the committee's decision to appoint you, Dr Barrymore,' he said. 'And you may as well know that you wouldn't have been my first choice. But, as I was unavoidably absent from your interview, I agreed to go along with my committee's choice.'

Lucinda drew in her breath. 'That makes me feel so welcome, Dr Rathbone!'

He gave her an enigmatic smile. 'I always believe in speaking my mind. . .'

'So I've noticed!'

'Ah, this is more like the girl I remember over the phone!'

'I'm not a girl, Dr Rathbone. I'm a twenty-seven-year-old doctor. If you didn't like my appointment you should have vetoed it. After all, you are the medical director of this hospital. It's not too late to call back one of the other candidates. . .'

'Please, Dr Barrymore.' He glanced down at the open file on his desk. 'May I call you Lucinda?'

'No, I don't think that would serve any purpose at all. I prefer to keep my professional and private image totally separate, Dr Rathbone.' She might as well burn her boats! From the steely glint in his eyes he looked as if he was going to dismiss her before she'd even started.

For a few moments there was an uneasy silence in the room. Lucinda saw a flicker of emotion in the director's hostile eyes before he glanced down once more at her open file. At length he spoke in a slow, measured tone.

'You certainly seem to have the right qualifications and experience for the job. Tell me, why did you want to move from St Celine's Hospital, which is after all one of the large teaching hospitals and, being situated in central London, is an ideal place for a young woman doctor to further her career? I wouldn't have thought that moving out here to the east of London would have appealed to you.'

She forced herself to smile, but her heart was pounding rapidly as she searched for the right words. 'I wanted to specialise in obstetrics, and the Mary Rathbone Hospital for Women and Children seemed an obvious choice.'

This was the reason she'd given the interview panel, and it was true. But she wasn't going to divulge her other reasons for wanting to come here. . .not yet!

The reply seemed to satisfy him. She'd hoped it would, having relied on the fact that he always gave the impression that his hospital was God's gift to the science of obstetrics. She supposed he could be justifiably proud of the place, since it was his mother, the famous but reclusive Dr Mary Rathbone, who had founded it before he was born.

He stood up and moved around the desk, perching on the corner only inches away from her. Lucinda imagined she could see the hostile waves flowing out of him towards her. But there was something else. . .something she couldn't put her finger on. . .a kind of electric current of excitement that intrigued her. She realised that she desperately wanted to work with this man, in spite of all their differences.

'I think you're going to be something of a challenge, Dr Barrymore,' he said quietly. 'But I'm prepared to take a chance.'

How magnanimous! She stood up, her blue eyes levelling with his as he lounged against the desk. She would have liked to tell him to go to hell, but she wanted the job. It was a perfect opportunity for her to gain first-class experience in obstetrics, and to implement her own ideas on the subject. Not to mention the burning personal question that had haunted her ever since she'd discovered that this was the hospital where she'd been born to a mother she had never seen.

She gave him a saccharine smile as she swallowed her pride. 'I'm glad you're prepared to take a chance. When would you like me to start?'

'You can settle yourself in this morning and start work this afternoon.'

Lucinda's startled expression gave her away. Only yesterday she had been on duty at St Celine's, and she'd hoped for a couple of days' rest at the very least.

He pulled himself to his full height, towering above her. 'I hope you've got lots of stamina, Dr Barrymore, because I can be an absolute slave-driver. To be honest, when I first saw you just now, my heart sank. You look much too fragile for the job. I shall expect you to prove me wrong.'

She turned away. God, the man was insufferable! Everything she'd ever heard about him was true. He was arrogant, patronising and—by his own admission—a slavedriver! He regarded her as a challenge; well, the feeling was mutual.

'I can assure you, I'm very tough,' she told him through clenched teeth.

He was smiling as he moved ahead of her to hold open the door, signifying that the interview was at an end. 'What you lack in stature you make up for in spirit.'

She smiled back at him. That was the first remotely complimentary utterance he'd made towards her.

'There's a Caesarian scheduled for two o'clock,' he told her abruptly. 'Theatre One; be there half an hour early. I'd like you to assist me.'

Talk about throwing you in at the deep end! Lucinda swallowed hard. 'Yes, sir.'

The 'sir' was a reflex action to a command from higher authority. As she uttered it, she could have bitten out her tongue. She was trying so hard not to give him the upper hand.

As she walked away down the long corridor, her feet echoing on the tiled floor, she reflected that the redoubtable Dr Jonathan Rathbone was probably congratulating himself on having won Round One. But she comforted herself with the knowledge that the contest had barely started!

Her room in the staff quarters was approached by an outside stone staircase from the main forecourt of the hospital. The strident sound of an ambulance hurtling up towards the main doors reminded her that living over the shop, so to speak, would give her little time for leisure. But she told herself that she didn't mind. She loved her job and was happier working than gaddling about in the bright lights of London. It wasn't her scene any more. . .not since Adrian had gone away.

She reached the top step and pushed open the door. A blast of warm air welcomed her into the staff reception area. A middle-aged secretary, sitting at a desk by the window that overlooked the forecourt, smiled as she approached.

'The porter has put your luggage in your room, Dr Barrymore. How did you enjoy your interivew with the boss?'

Lucinda laughed. 'I didn't!' She'd been grateful to this comfortable, motherly woman for her warmth and friendliness both at her initial interview with the panel and earlier that morning when she'd arrived, weighed down with the sum total of all her possessions.

Edith Jackson smiled, putting up her hand to check that her impeccable grey waves were still riding high. 'You'll soon change your tune. Jonathan Rathbone will have you eating out of his hand like everyone else.'

'You must be joking!'

'He's a superb obstetrician,' the older woman countered.

'I don't doubt it—that's partly why I came here. But he's too big-headed for words!'

'He has a right to be proud of what he's achieved. I must admit I was apprehensive when he took over on his mother's retirement eight years ago. He was so young—only thirty. But he soon showed us what he was made of. He had the place running like clockwork in no time.'

'I can imagine,' Lucinda observed drily. He was a clockwork sort of man. . .no heart!

'The patients adore him.' Miss Jackson was not to

be put off her eulogy in mid-flow. 'And all the nurses are in love with him.'

Lucinda grinned. 'That must make his life very difficult.'

'Oh, he never gives them any encouragement in that direction. It would hamper the smooth running of the hospital.'

'Of course.' Lucinda found she was enjoying herself! 'You sound as if you've been here a long time, Miss Jackson.'

'Oh, dear me, yes. I've been here. . .let me see. . .a good thirty years.'

Lucinda drew in her breath. 'Since before I was born.' Oh, if only she dared ask a few questions now! But she'd better keep her personal problems until she was more established. She'd waited a long time to find out about her natural mother. It could wait a little longer, she thought, as she moved off down the corridor.

Her room was sparsely but adequately furnished with two armchairs, a single bed and a desk. She discovered that there was even a tiny shower cubicle. What luxury! Her own en-suite facilities, as it said in all the travel brochures.

She crossed to the window and stood looking out across the grey scene. The first flakes of December snow were drifting aimlessly down to land as squelchy puddles on the pavement. People hurried past the main gates, their heads bowed against the cruel east wind, looking as though their minds were focused on the daily grind of making ends meet.

Lucinda turned back and looked around her

room, wondering how long she would stay here. Her contract was for six months, renewable on mutual agreement. It wasn't likely that Jonathan Rathbone would want to keep her on after she'd insisted on making the changes she planned!

But it was something she had to do, and she wasn't afraid of putting her job on the line. She felt very strongly that all women should be able to choose their method of delivery. They shouldn't be categorised and dictated to. And from her own experience of Jonathan Rathbone she had formed the opinion that he was anything but pliable on the subject. There had been the case of her old school friend, for instance. Julia had desperately wanted a natural birth, but had the great man listened? Oh, no! Julia had been rushed into theatre as soon as she arrived here and the baby was delivered by Caesarian section. One day she'd tackle him on that one.

She spent the rest of the morning settling into her room before heading back into hospital to try out the medical haute cuisine. As she tasted the delicious steak and kidney pie, which had been waitress-served at a table with an immaculate white tablecloth, she found herself impressed. The Rathbone family certainly seemed to take care of their staff!

She was joined at the table by a couple of intense-looking women doctors who glanced in her direction and gave her a brief nod before immersing themselves back in their conversation. Halfway through the pie she felt a hand on her shoulder and looked up in surprise. Her colleagues at the table were looking over her head and smiling ingratiatingly. She turned and looked up into the dark brown eyes of her boss.

'I want you to come now. We've got to do the Ceasar stat!'

Lucinda swallowed the delicious morsel and stood up. From the intense look on Jonathan Rathbone's face she could tell this was a real emergency. In her time at St Celine's as a junior house surgeon, she'd got used to partially eaten meals.

As she followed Jonathan Rathbone along the corridor she was desperately trying to keep up with his long strides. His taunts about her fragility still smarted!

He swept through the swing doors of the ante-theatre, not waiting to see if she was still in tow.

'And next time, I hope you'll be wearing your bleeper, Dr Barrymore,' he flung over his shoulder. 'I don't want to have to nursemaid you along for every emergency.'

Ninety-nine, one hundred! She was still counting, and her fury remained unabated. If the wretched man had issued her with a bleeper she would have been wearing one, she thought, as she scrubbed furiously at her hands.

A nurse came up behind her and secured the fastenings on her green theatre gown. The first theatre cap that was produced proved to be much too large, and the nurse was sent scurrying away by Theatre Sister to find an 'extra small one'.

She daren't even look to see if her boss had noticed the delay. But when she went through into Theatre One, he looked across the table and said,

'Are you sure you're quite happy with that cap, Dr Barrymore? Perhaps you'd like us to postpone the operation while you have your hair done.'

'Maybe you'd like to fill me in on the details of the case,' she said evenly. 'I was hoping to be familiar with the case before we started.'

'There's no time. I'll fill you in as we go along. I'm in charge, so you don't need to worry your pretty little head too much. Just do as I tell you.'

CHAPTER TWO

LUCINDA watched Jonathan Rathbone's gloved hand making the first incision in the lower abdomen of their anaesthetised patient.

'Hold the retractors steady, Dr Barrymore!' he barked as he bent lower to inspect the uterus.

Lucinda froze as she reflected that she couldn't be steadier if she were a statue!

'I'm going to make an incision into the lower segment of the uterus,' her boss intoned in a typical lecture-hall voice.

Out of the corner of her eye Lucinda could see a couple of medical students standing by the wall, hanging on to the great man's every word.

'The reason for the urgency of this case will become obvious as I proceed. The patient, Mrs Linda Johnson, first came to me at thirty weeks with a history of painless vaginal bleeding. On examination, I found that the lie of the foetus was unstable and the presenting part couldn't be made to engage in the pelvis. Dr Barrymore will explain what condition this would indicate.'

Lucinda swallowed hard. How dared he put her on the spot like this, with absolutely no previous contact with the patient! 'It would seem to indicate that the placenta was lying wholly or partially in the lower uterine segment. . .' she began.

'Yes, yes, that's obvious,' interrupted her boss impatiently. 'But what are the implications?'

She stared at him coldly across the top of her mask. 'I was about to explain that as the lower segment stretches during the latter weeks of pregnancy, it's inevitable that there will be some separation of the placenta which will give rise to bleeding from the placental site. . .the condition we refer to as placenta praevia.'

'Very good, Dr Barrymore. I couldn't have put it better myself,' observed the suave obstetrician.

She controlled the urge to tell him not to patronise her. She wasn't one of his students!

'As this case is totally new to me,' she began carefully, 'perhaps, Dr Rathbone, you would explain what's been happening to our patient since the thirtieth week. From the clincial signs I would say that Mrs Johnson is almost full term.'

'Thirty-eight weeks, to be exact. Our patient has been here since the thirtieth week under close observation. I had hoped a normal delivery might be possible, but an hour ago, my examination revealed extensive bleeding. An immediate Caesarian was indicated.'

The obstetrician paused and took a deep breath as he reached into the uterus. 'And here, ladies and gentlemen, is our latest recruit for the baby unit. . .and it's a little. . .boy! And as far as I can see, he's quite perfect.'

A murmur of excited voices buzzed round the operating theatre.

'Now come along, folks. That's not the end, that's

the beginning. Here you are, Sister, take care of him. The usual routine. Make sure he gets plenty of the tender loving care you nurses are so good at.'

'Yes, sir.'

Theatre Sister beamed with happiness as she took the tiny bundle from the obstetrician, who was already totally absorbed in checking out the mother's uterus.

Lucinda held the sterile swabs steady between her forceps. Her heart was full as it always was at the moment of every new birth. There was something thrilling about the transformation of an unknown foetus into a tangible living baby. From the squalls and cries in the background it seemed their new addition was in good health. Tender loving care was what Jonathan Rathbone had ordered. She could just imagine him writing the letters TLC on the baby's chart, and she found herself surprised that such a technologically inspired man would even think of considering what he must surely think was an outmoded concept. It smacked of the old days of the midwife arriving on her bicycle with her little black bag.

'You can suture the abdominal wall, Dr Barrymore,' he instructed.

'Certainly, sir,' she replied, with a calmness she didn't feel.

She willed her hands not to tremble as he watched her. He was deliberately trying her out. . .trying to see what she was made of. . .

'There's no need to go in for all that embroidery.

Just the normal sutures you learned all those years ago when you were a mere medical student.'

Lucinda thought she heard suppressed titters from the side of the theatre as she worked on, with scrupulous care.

Jonathan Rathbone bent over as he watched her. Their heads were almost touching and she experienced an unusual feeling of urgent excitement. She suddenly realised that this arrogant man was actually capable of interesting her in a physical way.

'Not bad. . .not bad at all,' he murmured, so that only she could hear.

She looked up and their eyes met across the patient. Her pulses were unaccountably racing. She put it down to the heightened tension in the theatre at the safe delivery of the infant who had been in mortal danger. Yes, that was what it was. What else could it be? Jonathan Rathbone was the last man on earth she would fancy.

The patient was being wheeled out of the theatre, and she looked across enquiringly. 'Will that be all, sir?'

He smiled. 'Of course. My theatre sister is well organised. She's almost as much a slaverdriver as I am.'

'Which is saying a lot,' she said quietly, not knowing whether she wanted him to hear or not. Suddenly she didn't care what he thought of her. She'd passed the first test and acquitted herself very well.

She pulled off her cap as she went out through the swing doors, aware that he was right behind her. His hand suddenly reaching out to touch her shoulder sent a little shiver down her spine.

'Come and have a coffee.'

She looked up into the dark brown eyes and reassured herself that he was now in a friendly mood. His chiselled, aristocratic features seemed to have relaxed and she found his general expression not totally unappealing.

'Why not?' she replied, with just the right amount of cool. . .or so she judged! 'I'm terribly thirsty. I was just about to reach for a glass of water when you dragged me away from my lunch.'

'Yes, I'm sorry about that.'

He'd actually said he was sorry! Lucinda drew in her breath, enjoying the new-found rapport of two colleagues who had successfully concluded a difficult operation.

'Come along to my room when you've changed,' he added. 'I make better coffee than we get in the dining-room.'

She nodded, feeling sure that everything he did would be better than the norm. What a conceited man! She turned into one of the shower cubicles off the ante-theatre, peeled away her green theatre gown and threw it into the bin. But as the water splashed down over her body she found herself admitting that he was a good surgeon. He'd handled the case expertly. She wouldn't have done it any differently.

She smiled to herself. Perhaps she too was suffering from a touch of conceit. Maybe it was an obstetrician's disease. . .arrogance, or the art of knowing that you were always right! Perhaps it was because the very nature of the work they did made them strive for perfection. You couldn't make a mistake when the life of both mother and child depended on you.

She felt refreshed as she stepped out along the corridor in her freshly laundered white coat towards her boss's room. He opened the door when she knocked lightly and stood looking down at her appraisingly.

'I'm glad you're not one of those women who take forever to change,' he told her, standing back so that she could pass under his arm.

She laughed. 'I've never had the time to indulge myself in the luxury of pampering myself. My father taught me from an early age that time was a precious commodity. Something you didn't waste.'

He smiled as he handed her a cup of coffee and motioned her towards an armchair by the window. 'I presume your father must be a high-powered individual.'

'No, he was a very gentle man. He was a vicar who took his job very seriously. Nothing was ever too much trouble.'

'Was?' he queried.

'He died five years ago,' Lucinda said quietly.

'I'm sorry. And your mother?'

She took a sip of her coffee. 'She died last year.'

'Do you have any brothers or sisters?' he asked, in a surprisingly gentle voice.

She shook her head. 'Not that I know of.'

He gave her a quizzical look.

Lucinda took a deep breath. 'I was adopted at birth. . .and I don't know anything about my natural parents.'

He put down his cup and walked across the room to stand beside her chair. 'Have you ever wanted to get in touch with them? It's legal now for adoptees to be able to see their birth certificates. Sometimes we advise it here when we want to find out the family medical history of a patient.'

'I know all about that,' she said, wishing once more that he wouldn't patronise her. 'But I want to find out the real reason why my mother had me adopted before I take steps to contact her. I would hate to embarrass her. She probably has her own family and. . .' She broke off as she realised that her voice had been charged with emotion.

'It's obviously something you feel very strongly about, so I won't pry.' He moved away and stood looking out of the window.

'I don't mind at all,' she began carefully. Oh, how could she phrase the words? 'In actual fact. . .'

There was a knock at the door. Jonathan Rathbone moved across the room with a polite, 'Excuse me.'

Lucinda's heart was thumping madly. Perhaps it was going to be easier than she'd thought to gain the information about her birth at this hospital. Her boss seemed all in favour of adoptees knowing about their natural parents. It was a pity they'd been interrupted just now. But she would carry on where she'd left off as soon as she could. Impatiently she watched him opening the door.

'Mother!' he exclaimed. 'What are you doing here?'

Lucinda felt a wave of apprehension sweeping over her. This could only be the formidable, some would say legendary Dr Mary Rathbone. She remembered reading about this great philanthropist when she was still at school!

A tall, thin lady, her white hair swept back into a chignon, hurried into the room, her bright, intelligent eyes narrowing as they took in the cosy scene. 'This used to be my office. Why shouldn't I be here?'

Lucinda got to her feet as the old lady crossed the room. Dr Mary Rathbone had a certain regal presence that struck awe into younger members of the medical profession.

'Are you our new recruit?' she asked Lucinda in a sharp voice.

Jonathan Rathbone strode quickly across the room. 'Allow me to do the introductions. This is Dr Lucinda Barrymore; my mother, Dr Mary Rathbone.'

Lucinda swallowed hard. 'I'm delighted to meet you, Dr Rathbone. . .'

'Call me Dr Mary. It saves confusion. There've been so many Dr Rathbones in the family. My father, Dr Jeremiah Rathbone, whose legacy enabled me to found this hospital in 1947, insisted I keep my maiden name and pass it on to my son.'

The old lady paused for breath and sank down into an armchair next to Lucinda. Her son handed her a cup of coffee. As she took a sip, her shrewd eyes were still studying Lucinda.

'I came here specifically to meet you, Dr Barrymore,' she continued in an authoritative voice. 'I very rarely venture into the hospital these days. But I heard that your appointment had been made without my son being one of the interview panel and I wanted to see you for myself.' She paused briefly before enquiring, 'What do you make of her, Jonathan?'

Lucinda drew in her breath sharply. The old lady was as arrogant as her son. How dared they discuss her as if she were a candidate for a Miss World competition! She stood up abruptly.

'I'm afraid I can't stay. Thank you for the coffee, Dr Rathbone.' She turned at the door. 'It was a pleasure to meet you, Dr Mary.'

There was a frown on the old lady's face. Obviously it wasn't done to cut short an audience with the Queen! She should have waited to be dismissed.

'I'm going to check on our Caesarian case,' she explained, as if in mitigation. On reflection, she realised that it would be unwise to annoy Dr Mary. She might be retired, but she probably still had a great deal of influence. And there was the matter of gaining information about her natural mother. Dr Mary should have all the answers to that one.

'Come to supper this evening,' Dr Mary said in a voice that brooked no refusal. 'Jonathan will bring you. Seven-thirty sharp.'

Her boss was frowning. 'Are you sure it won't tire you, Mother? You know you don't like entertaining in the evening. It's a long time since. . .'

'Who's talking about entertaining?' the old lady retorted. 'A quiet little family supper is all I'm planning. Mrs Banks can surely manage to set another place at the table. It's been far too long since I had a guest in the evening. And besides, the girl intrigues me. I'm sure I've seen her somewhere before.'

Lucinda stood rooted to the spot, as Dr Mary's pale, watery eyes stared at her.

'Have we met before, Dr Barrymore?' the old lady asked. 'My memory isn't what it used to be, but I never forget a face.'

Jonathan Rathbone was holding open the door, a polite yet bored expression on his face. He bent down and whispered in Lucinda's ear, 'You'd better go now or you'll be here all day! Mother's nearly eighty and she's met a lot of people in her time. She's always imagining that someone reminds her of someone she knew a long time ago.'

'Speak up, Jonathan! I can't hear you,' Dr Mary snapped.

'I was saying that this is the first time Dr Barrymore has been to the hospital—apart from the interview—so it's unlikely you've seen her before, Mother.'

Lucinda opened her mouth to contradict him, but thought better of it. This wasn't the time to ask Dr Mary if she'd been the obstetrician who had brought her into the world! Her own face must have changed considerably in twenty-seven years. But perhaps she resembled her natural mother. Suddenly she couldn't wait for the evening to come. Supper with the woman who held the key to discovering her origins! It was all going so smoothly.

'Thank you for the invitation, Dr Mary. I shall look forward to this evening,' she said politely. As she looked up into Dr Jonathan Rathbone's eyes she saw a look of displeasure. Perhaps he didn't approve of his mother being familiar with the staff. Maybe the Rathbone dynasty usually kept themselves aloof from lesser mortals!

Dr Mary's face creased into a smile, giving the numerous wrinkles a softer look. 'And I shall look forward to it, my dear. Don't be late,' she added in a gruff voice. 'I can't abide unpunctuality.'

'Go and check on our patient,' Jonathan Rathbone said quickly. 'I'll be along in a few minutes.'

'Yes, sir.' Lucinda turned away and walked off down the corridor with a light step. It was worth playing the subservient woman if she was going to get her own way in the end!

As she passed a laundry bin on wheels standing outside the ward door, she had a sudden impulsive desire to jump on the metal bar and scoot off down the corridor just as she'd once done when she was a medical student. She smiled to herself as she remembered how she'd almost collided with her professor of surgery. He most definitely had not been amused!

'High spirits, Miss Barrymore, are all very well in their place,' he'd told her, 'but you'll have to curb them when you join our most revered profession. Does this tendency for high jinks run in your family?'

Lucinda remembered how she had stood awkwardly in front of him, hating to admit she didn't know what ran in her family. So she had given him the ambiguous answer, 'I expect so, sir.'

Now, as she avoided the trolley and pushed open the swing doors, she curbed the surge of excitement that was welling up inside her at the prospect of the revealing evening ahead. Meanwhile, she would do what she always did, concentrate on her work and put all personal thoughts out of her mind until later.

Her Caesarian patient, Linda Johnson, was cradling the newborn baby in her arms. She looked up at Lucinda and gave a smile of relief. 'I've been trying to feed him, Doctor, but I don't think he's getting very much.'

'Let me make you more comfortable, Mrs Johnson,' Lucinda said gently, as she pressed a pillow into the young mother's back. 'No, don't try to sit up. You can feed lying down. I expect your tummy's a bit sore.'

The patient gave a wry smile. 'You can say that again! But I didn't want to complain in front of the nurses. They've got their job to do, and I didn't want to be difficult. I've caused enough trouble as it is.'

'Nonsense! Complain all you like. That's what we're here for. . .to make life easier for you young mums.'

'Is there a problem, Dr Barrymore?'

She heard Dr Rathbone's deep voice coming from somewhere above her head. 'No problem at all, sir,' she replied, without turning round. 'Mrs Johnson was struggling to feed her baby without adequate help. What's the policy here on breast-feeding? I would have thought we could spare a nurse to help the new mums, especially the ones who've had a Caesarian. They should always be encouraged to feed in a reclining posture for the first few days.'

'It's a little difficult to allocate a nurse for each mother, Dr Barrymore,' said Jonathan Rathbone evenly. 'Look around you. Do you see the nurses standing around doing nothing? They bring the infants to the mothers, check that they know how to feed and return to collect them in due course. Mrs Johnson isn't new to breast-feeding. It's her third baby.'

'It's her first Caesarian,' Linda countered quietly. 'What happened to the tender loving care you ordered?'

She saw the pallor beneath her boss's healthy tan and sensed the indignation seething below the suave veneer. Probably he wasn't used to being challenged. Well, he would have to get used to it now that she was on his staff! Perching herself on the edge of the bed, she put her hand under the baby's head to support it as it sucked eagerly on its mother's nipple.

She dared not raise her eyes to look at her boss, but she was very much aware that he was watching her. After a few seconds she heard him moving away.

'Let me know when you've finished, Dr Barrymore,' he said, in a strained voice. 'I'd like to examine the abdomen.'

Lucinda smiled, but kept her eyes studiously on her patient and the tiny infant. 'Certainly, sir.'

Linda Johnson gave a sigh. 'Isn't he gorgeous?'

'Who? Your baby? Yes, I think. . .'

'No, I mean Dr Rathbone!' the patient laughed. 'Well, I mean my baby's lovely, of course, but between you and me and the gatepost, I really fancy that doctor. I think he's quite sweet on Sister Bradwell. Look, he's talking to her now.'

Lucinda raised her head and looked across towards Sister's desk. Jonathan Rathbone had draped his tall frame across the end of the desk and was bestowing a charming smile on the obviously besotted sister.

'I think you could be right, Mrs Johnson,' she agreed.

'Oh, do call me Linda. I may have three kids, but I'm still only twenty-three. And if I didn't have a husband I'd set my cap at that hunk of manhood over there. Is he married?'

Lucinda took the now satiated infant away from his mother's breast and was rewarded with a little burp as she rubbed the tiny back. 'I've no idea whether or not he's married,' she replied.

She was about to add that she wouldn't imagine any woman on earth could put up with his insufferable arrogance, but she decided against it. It was better to allow the patients their hero-worship even if it was misplaced.

She drew in her breath as she saw him coming back across the ward, his long strides echoing on the polished floor.

'Finished, Dr Barrymore?' he enquired, with a forced smile.

'Yes; you can take over, Dr Rathbone. What did Sister say about the feeding arrangements?'

She saw him hesitate and wondered if he'd even taken the trouble to mention it.

'Sister Bradwell says she'd like to discuss it with you, but in the meantime she'll continue as usual. We've worked together for a number of years without any complaints. There seems no reason to change the system just because someone is dying to try out their new broom and sweep us clean away.'

Linda smiled. 'I'll go and discuss it with Sister Bradwell now.'

'It's not convenient at the moment. She's about to take her tea break.'

She started to move away. 'This won't take long. I'm sure she can spare me a few minutes.'

'Dr Barrymore!'

She turned round and met his eyes with a bland stare. 'Yes, Dr Rathbone?'

He moved towards her so that the patient would be out of earshot. Then, lowering his voice, he spoke to her through clenched teeth.

'I would prefer you leave the matter until a more convenient time. And that's an order!'

Lucinda found her breathing was increased as she stared up into his blazing eyes. It was almost impossible to swallow the angry retort that welled up inside her. But suppress it she did, with difficulty! If this was the way the captain wanted to run his ship then it was pointless arguing with him. But he would get no loyalty from her. She'd stay just as long as was necessary to accomplish her objectives and then she'd tell him what he could do with his job! And she would really relish that situation!

'Whatever you say, Dr Rathbone,' she said, giving him a sweet smile. 'Just so long as the patients receive the best care possible. If your rigid rules work, then stick to them, by all means. But I do believe that my new broom might be useful even in these hallowed halls.'

'I may as well tell you that I don't like your attitude,' he hissed softly. 'And I think it would be better if you sent a message to my mother telling her that you're unable to come to supper this evening. You can telephone the housekeeper and. . .'

'Oh, but I wouldn't like to disappoint an old lady,' she broke in, with a wide ingenuous smile. 'Seven-thirty, was it?'

She turned and left him standing in the middle of the ward as she hurried after the departing sister.

'Sister Bradwell,' she called, in a deliberately pleasant voice, 'may I have a word?'

CHAPTER THREE

LUCINDA'S heart was in her mouth as she climbed up the stone steps of the imposing Rathbone residence. It was set back from the hospital, in grounds that looked as though they belonged to a stately home. Opulent just wasn't the word for the place. . .palatial perhaps? As she placed her hand on the highly polished brass door knocker, she found herself wondering why an old lady would want to live on in a place that looked for all the world like a glorified museum. Maybe it held happy memories for her; maybe. . .

'Yes?'

Lucinda decided that the woman who had just poked her head round the door must be doubling as head cook and bottle-washer because of the harassed look on her face and the nervous wiping of her wet hands down the front of her apron.

'I'm Dr Lucinda Barrymore,' she began. 'Dr Mary is expecting me.'

'They get younger,' the housekeeper observed, peering over the top of her pince-nez. 'You'd better come in. . .wipe your feet. I've just done this floor.'

Lucinda stepped into the impressive high-ceilinged, oak-panelled hall, her feet echoing on the highly-polished floor when she'd finished her dutiful session on the doormat.

'They're in the sitting-room. What would you like to drink?' she was asked abruptly.

'Oh, whatever the. . .er. . .family are drinking.'

'Dr Mary doesn't on account of her liver and Dr Jonathan drinks whisky, which will be too strong for a young girl like you, so I'll bring you a glass of sherry,' said the housekeeper.

'Thank you, that will be. . .'

Lucinda realised she was talking to herself as the housekeeper hurried off into the nether regions of the house, having first pushed open the sitting-room door with a peremptory, 'Visitor for you.'

Nervously Lucinda stepped inside the room. Mother and son were seated on either side of the fireplace, where the flames from a roaring log fire were licking up the chimney. They were both engrossed in their respective books, and Lucinda felt like an intruder come to break up the peace of the evening. Oh, God! What on earth had made her come? She knew she wasn't welcome.

Jonathan Rathbone put down his book on the Sheraton side table and got to his feet with studied languor.

'So you came, after all, Dr Barrymore,' he observed evenly.

She forced herself to smile, as much to calm her nerves as a desire to ingratiate herself. 'Yes, I came. Good evening, Dr Mary.' She moved towards the old lady, sensing that it would be better to ally herself to the mother rather than the son.

'Sit here, my dear,' said Dr Mary, patting the

chair beside her. 'You look tired. Have you been busy?'

Lucinda risked a look across the fireside at her boss. Oh, yes, she'd been busy! Busily changing the feeding routine with Sister Bradwell, who had gone along with most of the new ideas she had put forward after her first initial hesitancy. She wondered how long before Jonathan Rathbone would haul her over the coals about it.

'Just a routine sort of day,' she replied easily. 'I'm beginning to find my feet. The first day is always the most difficult.'

'Only if you deliberately set out to make it so,' Jonathan Rathbone murmured under his breath.

'What was that?' asked Dr Mary. 'I do wish you'd speak up.'

'I was asking our guest if she'd like a drink.'

'Of course she'd like a drink. So would I, but it wouldn't like me. Ah, here it comes.' Dr Mary smiled up at her housekeeper. 'You can serve the supper in a few minutes, Hilda.'

Lucinda accepted her sherry. As she sipped it she found her eyes drawn to the portraits on the wall behind Jonathan Rathbone's head. Suddenly she realised that it looked as if she were staring at him. Nervously she averted her eyes.

'I was just admiring the portraits,' she explained, and took another gulp of sherry. A warm glow suffused her oesophagus, and when she looked across the fireplace again she decided that her boss could be quite appealing if you liked conceited men.

He got to his feet. 'Come and have a look at them. It's like the rogues' gallery.'

'It's nothing of the kind!' protested his mother.

Lucinda glanced at the old lady and saw that she was smiling affably.

'Our illustrious ancestors!' Dr Rathbone announced with a dramatic sweep of his arm.

Lucinda was now standing close beside him looking up at the portraits, and she was desperately aware that the top of her head only reached up to his shoulder. Whoever it was who'd said that it was charming to be only as high as a man's heart was an idiot! At that moment, she wished she had long legs so that she could look this arrogant man in the eye. Instead of which she found herself craning her neck to get a better look at the portraits. At one point she even imagined he was going to pick her up and hold her in front of the wall, as if she were a child.

'You can't see that top one very well, but that's my grandfather, Jeremiah Rathbone,' he told her.

'The one who left the legacy for the founding of the hospital,' she supplied, remembering what Dr Mary had told her that afternoon.

'The very one. And this was my father.'

She looked up at the handsome face of a young officer in Air Force uniform. 'Was he a doctor?'

'Of course. But he was killed in a plane crash just before I was born, so I never knew him.'

Lucinda was chilled by the matter-of-fact tone he used and found herself wondering how he could be so unemotional. She glanced across at Dr Mary and saw that she too was undisturbed by the disclosure.

'Supper is served, Dr Mary.' The housekeeper stood in the doorway, perspiration on her round pink face as if she'd just straightened up from delving into the oven.

Lucinda felt Jonathan Rathbone's hand under her elbow, and the touch of his fingers unnerved her momentarily. She caught a waft of expensive after-shave that showed he was definitely in an off-duty mood. And she suddenly found herself wondering if he had put it on to impress her. He certainly wouldn't have put it on just for an evening by the fireside with his mother.

Dr Mary had hurried ahead to check on the dining-room. As Lucinda walked beside her boss down the long corridor, she was very much aware of him as a man. She realised that she'd never thought of him in a sexual context. Over the phone, between hospitals, he had simply been a sparring partner. . .and a particularly belligerent one at that! But now, seeing him here in his home background, in a softer, more gentle mood, she could begin to realise what the nurses and patients saw in him.

'This way, Dr Barrymore,' he directed her quietly.

She glanced up at him as she felt the tightening of his fingers under her arm. The outline of his features against the romantic candlelit setting of the dining-room made her quite forget her aversion. She wondered if perhaps, just for tonight, she should dispense with her preconceived ideas about the man.

He gave her a slow, enigmatic smile, as if he too was reconsidering his first impressions. 'Sit here, Dr Barrymore.'

He was pulling out a chair at the end of the long table, and she tried to sit down as elegantly as possible. Suddenly, she had found that the opulent atmosphere of the room was making her nervous. A little family supper was how Dr Mary had described the evening. Did they really always eat like this, in a candlelit room, at a gleamingly polished table, with an array of antique silver cutlery that wouldn't look out of place in a royal palace?

Dr Mary had eased herself into the chair that Jonathan had held out for her, and Lucinda watched as her boss took his place at the head of the table, flanked by the two of them.

'Your name is Lucinda, isn't it?' Dr Mary said, her eyes staring intensely across the table. 'I think we'll dispense with the Doctor title tonight.' She turned to look at her son. 'You've no objections, have you, Jonathan?'

A boyish grin suffused his features, making him look much younger than the stern consultant that Lucinda had got used to.

'I think you'll find that Dr Barrymore prefers to keep her title,' he began. 'For some reason. . .'

'Please, call me Lucinda!' she put in hurriedly, as she realised that her initial attempt at keeping her distance now seemed so churlish.

The housekeeper placed a large antique tureen of soup in front of Dr Mary, handing her mistress a china ladle as if it were a surgical instrument.

'Thank you, Hilda, I can manage,' the old lady said.

When Mrs Banks had gone back to the kitchen

and Dr Mary had served the delicious, home-made vegetable soup, Lucinda complimented her hostess on the efficiency of her housekeeper.

Dr Mary smiled. 'Mrs Banks used to be my theatre sister many years ago. After she retired, she asked if I could give her a job in the house. Her husband died when she was very young and she has no other family. In fact, she was born here when it was still a mother and baby home.'

'What a coincidence!' Lucinda paused in the middle of transferring the spoon to her mouth as she wondered if she'd really said that. Certainly she hadn't meant to get embroiled in the subject dearest to her heart so early in the evening. It must have been the relaxing effects of the sherry and the newfound warmth of her relationship with the Rathbones that had lulled her off guard.

Dr Mary's eyes narrowed. 'What's a coincidence?'

Lucinda put down her spoon and took a deep breath. 'According to my adoptive mother, *I* was born here. . .twenty-seven years ago last January. I was adopted straight from hospital. Were you in charge at that time, Dr Mary?'

The room suddenly seemed ominously quiet. Lucinda realised that mother and son were both staring at her.

Dr Mary frowned. 'Well, of course I was in charge. I ran the hospital from 1947 until my retirement. I suppose I must have had a hand in your adoption, but the name Barrymore doesn't ring a bell.'

'You told me your adoptive father was a vicar, didn't you?' put in Jonathan.

'Yes, but he was my adoptive mother's second husband. My first adoptive father was called Wilkinson. . . James Wilkinson. He was a barrister and. . .'

'I don't remember him at all.'

Lucinda stared across the table at her hostess, feeling puzzled at the unhelpful tone of voice. 'That's not surprising, Dr Mary. You must have dealt with so many cases, and twenty-seven years is a long time to remember a name. Would it be possible for you to look in your files and. . .?'

'That's totally out of the question. My records are sacrosanct.'

The cold voice shrivelled Lucinda's hopes of an easy solution. She could see that she was treading on very dangerous ground.

'I'm not suggesting that you should reveal anything that doesn't concern me, Dr Mary. But surely. . .'

'You must apply to the appropriate authorities through the usual channels. I understand it's possible now for adoptees to see their original birth certificates.'

'Yes, but I would prefer to know something of my background before I try to contact my natural mother,' Lucinda explained.

'You intend to try to contact your natural mother?' There was no disguising Dr Mary's profound disapproval.

Lucinda swallowed hard.'Yes, I do, as a matter of

fact. It would be nice to know what sort of a woman she was and why she had to give me up for adoption.'

'I would strongly advise against it! Let sleeping dogs lie. Nothing can be achieved by digging up the past,' the old lady retorted bitterly.

'But, Mother, it's sometimes advisable to understand the medical history of one's natural parents,' put in Jonathan Rathbone.

Lucinda flashed him a grateful smile. She hadn't dared to hope he would be on her side. Nor could she understand the resistance she was getting from Dr Mary. Surely the old lady couldn't deny the sense in what her own son was telling her?

'Do you have any medical problems, Lucinda?' Dr Mary stared at her guest with hostile eyes. 'Any problems that you might have inherited from your natural parents?'

Lucinda shook her head. 'No, I'm extremely healthy, but. . .'

'Then you should be content with your life as it is.' Dr Mary picked up a silver bell and rang furiously, signifying that there was nothing more to be said on the subject.

Lucinda tried to finish the last spoonfuls of her soup, but found that the altercation had soured her appetite. Some of it revived as she tasted the main course of saddle of lamb with mint sauce and perfectly cooked vegetables, but she was still puzzled by her hostess's unenlightened attitude.

There was a chocolate pudding dessert that looked delicious but which Lucinda declined. Only when they were settled back in the drawing-room with tiny china cups of strong black coffee did she dare to broach the subject again.

'I don't want to cause you any trouble, Dr Mary, but perhaps your son could instruct the Records Department to look into my case,' she said. 'I merely want to know if my natural mother would welcome being contacted by me. Surely the records will show the sort of background she has, and. . .?'

'I forbid it!' Dr Mary's eyes were gleaming with anger. 'I'm feeling very tired, so I'll bid you goodnight.'

Dr Jonathan had jumped to his feet to help his mother rise from her chair. It seemed to Lucinda that the old lady was leaning very heavily on her son's arm. She hadn't meant to upset her, but she could see that her questioning had caused distress.

'Goodnight, Dr Mary,' she said gently. 'I'm sorry if my visit has tired you.'

The old lady paused beside her chair and looked down into her eyes. Suddenly she put out her hand and touched Lucinda on the cheek. 'Leave it be, my child. There's no good in raking up the past. Live in the present. . .and look towards the future.'

Lucinda stared in surprise at the unexpected tears in Dr Mary's eyes and felt an icy shiver run down her spine. She was convinced the old doctor was remembering something. . .something about her own birth. But why was she withholding the information? Why was she so against Lucinda's search for the truth? What was there to hide?

She watched the old lady shuffling out of the room on the arm of her son. She seemed to have aged in the last few minutes. Lucinda felt even more determined to solve the enigma surrounding her birth, but she decided that she wouldn't trouble Dr Mary any further, whereas Dr Jonathan would surely give her some help. Without actually countermanding Dr Mary's orders they could make a few tentative enquiries. There were other people who had been around twenty-seven years ago. There was Edith Jackson, the medical secretary, and Hilda Banks, the ex-theatre sister.

Dr Jonathan briefly turned at the door. 'Don't go. . . I'll be back in a moment.'

Lucinda smiled as she settled back in her chair, reflecting that her boss's attitude was most encouraging.

She heard his feet in the corridor after several minutes. His absence had been longer than she had anticipated, and she wondered if his mother had proved difficult.

He stood in the doorway, his eyes searching her face.

'I hope I haven't upset your mother,' she began carefully.

He strode across the thick carpet and looked down at her. 'You mustn't broach the subject again. My mother is very. . .sensitive.'

'But why? Why is she sensitive about something which only affects me?' She realised that her voice had become high-pitched and urgent as her hands gripped the side of the Sheraton chair.

For an instant his eyes veiled over, and then suddenly he knelt down and took both of her hands in his own. She stared into the expressive eyes that were now level with her own and felt alarmed at the intensity of his gaze. His whole attitude had changed in the last few minutes since he had left the room with his mother. It was obvious to her that the old lady had confided in him, probably told him everything that she wanted to know, and he had been sworn to secrecy. She could feel the pressure of his fingers as they enveloped her own and a sensual warmth began to suffuse her body. It was a long time since she had been in such close contact with a man. Since Adrian had left her she had shunned the opposite sex like the plague. But now, with these strong surgeon's hands around her own, she felt a welcome relaxation stealing over her.

'I can't leave it like that,' she began hesitantly, unwilling to break up the easy rapport that had developed between them. Dr Mary had slammed the door in her face, but Jonathan Rathbone must surely see the urgency of her mission. Only minutes before, he had been supporting the idea of adoptees finding out about their origins.

'You must leave it,' he told her gently. 'I know it's hard for you, but you've got a good life, and nothing would be served by digging up the past.'

'You know something, don't you?' Lucinda challenged him.

She felt the increased pressure on her hands and drew in her breath as she waited for him to put her out of her misery.

Suddenly he pulled her to her feet and stood looking down at her with a tender expression. 'I can't answer that,' he replied quietly. 'You must judge for yourself.'

She wrenched away her hands and walked across to the fireplace, staring down into the dying embers that somehow seemed to signify the end of her hopes. 'Your mother must have remembered my adoptive father,' she persisted. James Wilkinson was an eminent QC in his time. Everyone knew him—he was knighted for his philanthropic works. Long after his death, when I was helping to clear out the attic, I found an old copy of *The Times* and there was an article on how he'd adopted me from the hospital here.'

'My mother only remembers the things she wants to nowadays. She has a useful knack of forgetting anything that might be remotely unpleasant,' he said carefully, coming up behind her and putting his hands on her shoulders.

She turned quickly and looked up into his eyes, thinking that a girl could happily drown in those expressive pools! There and then she made the resolution not to trouble him further with her personal problems. It was obvious that she would get no help at all. Her own efforts would have to be of a clandestine nature. And above all, she wanted to maintain this unexpected friendship that had sprung up between them. She could achieve more of her professional ambitions with this man as her ally.

'Let's forget the whole thing,' she said, forcing herself to smile as convincingly as possible.

She saw the relief in his eyes before she turned to move away. Unexpectedly, his grip tightened on her shoulders and she had to remain motionless. But the surprising thing was that she found herself welcoming the sensual touch of his hands.

'Thank you, Lucinda,' he whispered softly. 'Sometimes we have to deliberately forget. It's not always easy, but it's the only way to find peace of mind.'

She stared up at him, awed by the intensity of his voice. 'You sound as if you know what you're talking about,' she observed in a gentle tone.

He ran a hand through his black, wavy hair with an impatient gesture. 'Oh, yes, I've had to learn to forget,' he told her. 'I've had to learn to live in the present and think only about the future.'

'Would you care to talk about it?' she asked quietly.

She saw his brown, expressive eyes flicker with emotion, and for a split second she thought he was going to confide in her. But he merely smiled as he put a finger under her chin, tilting up her face towards his.

'I don't believe in opening up an old wound that's healed healthily.'

And then he bent his head, his lips brushing hers as lightly as a butterfly's wing.

CHAPTER FOUR

LUCINDA felt as if she would never get to sleep. The memory of his lips on hers kept haunting her. She remembered how he had pulled himself away, almost apologetically, and moved towards the door. He had made no reference to his tender kiss, making it seem like a momentary aberration.

But the annoying thing was that she couldn't stop thinking about it. She glanced at her luminous bedside alarm clock. Ye gods! It was three-thirty and she hadn't yet been to sleep. She told herself that she was behaving like a lovesick teenager instead of a responsible doctor with patients to care for in the morning.

She put on her bedside light and stared up at the ceiling as she wondered if Jonathan's kiss had the same effect on everyone. Did they all want to swoon into his arms, or did they have the sense to beat a hasty retreat as she'd done. . .and now wished she hadn't! Because it was so long since she'd felt remotely interested in the opposite sex. Adrian had put paid to so much of her emotion.

She closed her eyes, trying to blot out the unpleasant memories of that last evening when Adrian had told her, quite out of the blue, that their engagement was over. He was in love with someone else. She remembered how she'd known at once who that someone was! It didn't take a detective to realise that the girl was his consultant's daughter. Dr Adrian Matthews was desperately ambitious, and when his boss's daughter had started showing an interest in him, Lucinda had realised that she'd lost him to a calculated career move.

She turned over and lay on her side, watching the digital minutes tick by. She had suspected that Adrian's marriage to Fenella would only last as long as it was useful to him. Once he'd got the promotion he wanted he had begun to look around again. He had actually had the nerve to phone her and suggest they meet up again for old times' sake. She had slammed down the phone, after telling him she didn't go out with married men. But the thing that had most annoyed her was the fact that she'd allowed herself to be double-crossed in the first place. And, rather than trust her own judgement where men were concerned she had remained aloof for. . .how long was it now?. . .nearly five years.

She gave a deep sigh. Five years of her life with her emotions on ice. But now, after a brief kiss with a man she thought she disliked, she'd started warming up again.

Sleep, she told herself. That was what she needed, otherwise she would look such a fright in the morning, and that would never do. . .you never knew who you might meet on the wards. . .

The snowflakes were getting bigger and were actually beginning to settle when she looked out of the window. As she ran down the stairs to the dining-room, Lucinda wondered if they would have a white Christmas this year. Holly, mistletoe, presents under the tree. . .maybe Jonathan Rathbone would invite her over to his house and they would sit by the log fire and. . .

Quickly she checked her romantic thoughts. It was one thing to decide she could be friends with her boss and quite another to get a crush on him. She wasn't going to join the queue of starry-eyed young hopefuls.

Breakfast was a help-yourself affair set out on long tables that ran the length of the dining-room. But it was still a more civilised type of meal than Lucinda had become used to in the cramped canteen conditions of her previous hospital. Somehow the Rathbones had managed to stamp their aristocratic way of life around the place.

She smiled to herself as she settled down to her scrambled eggs, wondering how on earth the kitchen staff had produced such a delicious consistency in a dish that was always a test when large quantities were required. It couldn't have tasted better if the redoubtable Dr Mary herself had made it!

Talking of whom. . .Lucinda gazed across the dining-room in amazement as the erstwhile founder and director moved between the tables and beelined towards her. It was an automatic gesture to leap to her feet and hold out a chair for the old lady.

'Thank you, my dear,' Dr Mary said as she sank down and took several deep breaths to recover from her early morning activities. 'I don't usually come over to the hospital, as I told you yesterday, but I felt I had to see you again. . .and as soon as possible.'

A bewildered waitress hovered beside Dr Mary's chair, a nervous, ingratiating smile on her lips. 'May I bring you some breakfast, ma'am?' she asked in a nervous voice.

'Oh, good heavens, no, child. I'm here on a social visit. But I wouldn't say no to a cup of your excellent coffee. Still using the filters I gave you?'

'Yes, ma'am.'

'Good. Now run along and bring me a good strong cup. I've got to have some vices to brighten up my old age. Now, where was I?'

Lucinda swallowed hard. 'You were saying you wanted to see me, Dr Mary.'

'Yes, I couldn't sleep last night.'

'That makes two of us,' said Lucinda ruefully.

'Our argument affected you, then?'

'That and. . . I'm always disturbed by new jobs,' Lucinda added hastily.

'And that's the last thing I should want, my dear. I do so want you to be happy here. If I seemed unhelpful, it's because I've only got your best interests at heart. I've seen several disappointments between natural mothers and long-lost children, and my policy now is to discourage it. I wanted to make sure you understood.'

Lucinda smiled. 'But of course. I understand perfectly.' Far more than you realise! she thought.

The look of relief on the old lady's face made her feel guilty, but she appeased her conscience with the thought that Dr Mary was the one who was withholding information that was hers by right. She didn't want to cause her any further anxiety. She would simply make her own private enquiries and not disclose her findings to the Rathbones.

'This coffee is excellent,' Dr Mary was telling the waitress, who went away with a satisfied smile on her face.

Lucinda took a large gulp of hers as she saw her boss coming in through the wide-open oak doors. For one awful moment she thought she was going to blush. She hadn't blushed since she was at school and she wasn't going to start now, even though the memory of that unnerving kiss was still etched deeply in her mind.

He was towering above her now and she thought, inconsequentially, how handsome he looked in his morning-fresh white coat with his stethoscope slung round his neck. But she didn't like the stern expression on his face. . .no, she didn't like that one bit!

'Good morning, Mother. I didn't expect to see you in hospital again, and so early. Is anything the matter?' he asked, completely ignoring Lucinda.

'I came to see Lucinda,' his mother told him.

'That makes two of us. I've just been speaking to Sister Bradwell.'

'Ah!' Lucinda drew in her breath with a hissing sound. It was a bit early in the morning to start sparring with her boss, but she'd better make a plan of campaign. 'You see, it's like this,' she began carefully.

He waved his hand imperiously. 'No excuses, please.'

She got to her feet, craning her neck so that she could glare up at him. 'I assure you, you weren't going to get any.'

'I don't think we need to bother my mother with the boring details. Come to my office when you've finished your breakfast.' His voice softened as he glanced back at his mother. 'Do you need anything, Mother?'

'No, thank you, Jonathan. I'm going back home in a minute.'

Lucinda watched the white-coated figure striding away from her and felt glad that she'd totally exorcised the effect of his kiss. . .well, almost! He still cut a dashing figure as he swept out of the room, and she couldn't deny the fact that her pulses were racing. . .although that was probably with a righteous indignation, because she wasn't going to give way one inch on the feeding routine she'd got Sister Bradwell to agree to.

Dr Mary put down her cup and stood up, and Lucinda thought how erect the old lady was. She didn't look as if she was approaching eighty, or even seventy-eight. Doing a rapid calculation on what she had been told, she worked out that if she had retired eight years ago when she was seventy. . .

'Don't let my son drive you too hard, Lucinda,' the old lady said, as they walked out of the dining-room together. 'I'd like you to be happy here.'

Lucinda turned towards Dr Mary and was again surprised to see the tears welling up in her eyes. She felt a shiver of apprehension. Maybe she should take the old lady's advice and let sleeping dogs lie. Maybe she wouldn't like what she found out about her natural mother. But when her curiosity was aroused as it was now, she couldn't call a halt. She couldn't live the whole of her life under an ominous shadow of doubt.

'You're very kind,' she said quietly.

Dr Mary had turned away, so there was no way of knowing how she was reacting now. Lucinda heard her faint, 'Goodbye,' as she watched the old lady making her way down the corridor to the main door. 'Now for the lion's den!' she muttered under her breath.

Jonathan Rathbone was seated at his desk, his eyes unwavering from the medical report in front of him. Lucinda fumed silently as she waited for him to deign to raise his head.

'Now, what's all this about informal feeding?' he asked after a full two minutes had elapsed.

'Sister Bradwell has come round to my way of thinking on that one,' she told him, unable to restrain the note of triumph that crept into her voice.

'And what exactly do you intend the mothers to do? Shall I send out for an entertainments manager to keep them happy while they feed? Perhaps we could have a performing circus in the middle of the ward. . .'

'There's no need to take that tone with me. I only want what's best for our patients,' she countered quietly.

For an instant, you could have heard a pin drop. Lucinda waited with bated breath for the storm that would follow her mutinous declaration. But, to her amazement, it never came. And then, to her surprise, her boss stood up and came round the desk to sit on the edge of it, directly in front of her.

'Fire away,' he said solemnly. 'I'm all ears.'

She took a deep breath. 'I believe that mothers feed their infants better when they're fully relaxed, so we have to give them conditions as near like their own homes as possible. I've asked Sister Bradwell to have the old fireplace at the far end of the ward opened up. She will instruct one of the porters to light the fire each morning and place armchairs around it. . .'

'But many of our patients live in tower blocks,' her boss broke in, his hand sweeping back the recalcitrant waves that had fallen over his forehead. 'Ye gods, half of them have never seen an open fire!'

'Then it's time we rectified the matter,' she retorted swiftly. 'In the old days, the hearth was the centre of the home. All the women sat around chatting as they fed their babies, and there was a warm and relaxed attitude which was beneficial to the stimulation of the milk supply. No one had to go around chivvying them into action as if they were cows connected to an electric milking machine. We've got to get back to doing things the natural way. Mother Nature knows what she's doing, but we have to listen to her.'

She broke off, aware that her explanation had

turned into an impassioned plea. Risking a glance at her boss, she saw that his face had softened. Some of the rigid lines she had noted earlier had disappeared, and he had shed several years in the process.

He gave her a wry grin. 'It's going to be a great upheaval. Some of the nurses won't like it. They much prefer to keep the mums in their own cubicles.'

'Oh, I'm sure it will interrupt the smooth running of the hospital, but why are we here? Not to make life easy for the staff, I assure you. We're here for the convenience of the patients. To see that they remain happy, because a happy mother will produce a happy child.'

Jonathan was shaking his head, but there was an amused smile on his face. 'OK, I'll go along with it for a trial period. But if I get too many complaints from the staff or the patients I'll veto it.'

'Don't worry, you won't. Believe me, I've seen it work. When my father. . .my second adoptive father, the Reverend Mark Barrymore, took us out to Africa when I was a child, I used to help at the hospital mission. And when we tried to impose hospital routine on the patients their progress was impeded. But when we allowed them to roam freely and behave as if they were at home, they recovered and became healthy again.'

His smile broadened and he leaned forward, cupping her chin in his hand. She held her breath as she found her face only inches away from his eyes.

'So it's back to the jungle, is it? We throw out all our technological apparatus, do we?'

'I didn't say that. I said we should listen to the rhythm of the natural world.'

'You can be very persuasive, Lucinda.'

She stiffened as she heard him call her by her first name. It seemed somehow so out of place here in his office. And she was trying so hard to remain detached from him. . .which was proving impossibly difficult when he was looking deep into her eyes! She could feel her lips tingling where he'd kissed her only hours ago, and, quite out of the blue, came a desire for a repeat performance. . .only this time she'd like it to last a bit longer!

She moved her head away and stood up decisively. Even so, her head was only on a level with his as he remained lounging against the desk. 'I take it you approve if I go ahead and implement the new feeding plan now?' she queried, trying to ignore the rapid beating of her pulse.

Jonathan pulled himself to his full height. 'For a trial period only. . .let's say one month. Agreed?'

Lucinda smiled. 'Agreed!' She saw that he was holding out his hand as if to shake on an agreement of monumental importance. Steadily she held out her own and their hands closed around each other. The clasp was so different from the one she had experienced when she'd arrived the day before. It was so strange how you could change your opinion of a man in such a short time. She was beginning to think that she'd found out how to handle this man, and he wasn't as set in his medical ways as she had feared. In fact, he was proving to be positively amenable.

'Are you planning to introduce any more of your weird and wonderful ideas while you're with us?' he asked.

Lucinda hesitated. This wasn't the time to go into long details of her ideas on optional delivery methods. No, she'd better take just one step at a time. She wasn't sure how far she could trust him to approve her methods. He never had in the past when they had spoken over the telephone.

'Let's see how this little pilot scheme goes,' she answered ambiguously. 'Maybe there'll be one or two adjustments to routine that I'd like to make.'

He gave her a wary smile. 'You will make sure you check with me first, won't you?'

'Of course!' She flashed him a brilliant smile.

'And about last night, Lucinda. . .'

'What about it?' she broke in, a little more quickly than she'd meant to. The only thing she remembered about their evening together was the kiss. . .the monumental kiss that had turned her from a block of ice into a quivering mass of forgotten emotions.

'I'm sure you realise that my mother didn't mean to be harsh with you.'

She breathed a sigh of relief. . .or was it disappointment? At any rate, she now knew he'd forgotten about the kiss.

'No, of course she didn't,' she replied quickly. 'I understand that she was trying to protect me from something. I don't know what it is, but. . .' Her voice trailed away as she realised she'd been about to admit her intention to get to the bottom of the mystery. She took a deep breath before continuing,

'I don't know what it is, but I promise not to ask your mother any more questions.'

He seemed satisfied with her answer as he nodded his approval. 'It wouldn't do to upset her. She's much frailer than she likes to appear. Her early years of struggle took it out of her, though she doesn't like to admit it.'

Lucinda frowned. 'I find it difficult to imagine your mother struggling. Her lifestyle is so opulent that. . .'

'Don't be deluded by appearances,' he put in hurriedly.

She heard the harsh tone and noted the veiled expression in his eyes. Once again she felt he was holding something back from her, but she decided not to pry.

'I'm going to the wards,' she said briskly, turning away and heading for the door.

His long easy strides overtook her and he pulled open the door, to stand looking down at her with a bemused smile on his lips. 'Quite the little whirlwind!'

'Less of the little!' she admonished, with a playful smile. 'The most concentrated medicine always comes in small bottles.'

'Then please do me the honour of bringing your healing properties along while we do our round of the wards.'

She hurried along beside him, terribly aware of the envious looks of some of her new colleagues as they passed them in the corridor. Jonathan was chatting amiably to her as if they were the best of friends, but she had the awful feeling that this friendship was a fragile thing. It couldn't last, not with the differences between them, but she would enjoy it while she could.

She listened to and assisted her boss as they did the rounds, constantly aware of the esteem in which he was held. She would have to be careful not to do anything to break up the relationship the great man had forged between his staff and his patients. But not at the expense of her own interests. There were so many things she wished to achieve here, and she only had six months in which to do it.

They checked the new mothers and their infants, including their Caesarian patient, Linda Johnson. Her tiny baby boy seemed to be thriving and there were no post-natal problems.

As they moved on, Sister Bradwell came down the ward, a nervous expression on her face.

'I'm glad to find the two of you together. I thought we could have a chat. Would you care to come into my office for some coffee?' she asked.

'I expect you want to sound me out about Dr Barrymore's weird and wonderful ideas, don't you, Sister?' smiled Jonathan.

'Well, actually, sir. . .'

'Don't worry, she's told me all about your little discussion. I must say, I thought you might have been more conservative. Dr Barrymore is convinced that this is the hospital where Florence Nightingale still wanders with her lamp!'

Sister Bradwell's eyes showed her confusion. 'Are you saying you agree or disagree, sir?'

'I disagree in principle, but I'll agree in practice,' he replied, his sardonic eyes sweeping from one to the other. 'Do whatever you ladies think is best. Sorry I haven't the time for coffee, Sister, but I'm sure my colleague could do with a cup.'

He turned at the door and spoke quietly to Lucinda. 'Perhaps you could report back to me on the outcome. How about this evening? Shall we say eight-thirty? I'll pick you up from the staff quarters.'

Lucinda opened her mouth to reply, but Jonathan Rathbone had disappeared through the swing doors.

'You lucky thing!' breathed Cynthia Bradwell under her breath. 'He seems to have taken a fancy to you.'

Lucinda drew in her breath sharply. 'I'm not so sure. It could simply be a calculated move to keep me toeing the line.'

But she hoped it wasn't!

CHAPTER FIVE

JONATHAN RATHBONE was waiting for her by the desk in the foyer of the staff quarters when she arrived promptly at eight-thirty. The secretary, Edith Jackson, working late at her desk, looked up with a knowing smile.

'Going out on the town, are we?'

'And why not?' Jonathan Rathbone said, with a boyish grin. 'I'm sure you can hold the fort until we get back, Edith.'

'Yes, but I'd like to know where you're going,' the middle-aged stalwart replied. 'It's one of the perks of my job—knowing all about who's going out with whom, where they're going and for what nefarious purpose.'

The consultant bent his head and scribbled something on the secretary's notepad. 'It's all there, so you'll be able to have vicarious pleasures all evening.'

Edith Jackson's smile broadened as she glanced down to see what her boss had written. 'My, I'm impressed!' She turned to look at Lucinda. 'He doesn't take everyone to his favourite restaurant. He's either planning to seduce or sack you.'

Dr Rathbone gave a boyish grin. 'You see how Edith has been studying my tactics since I was still at school? She thinks she knows all about me.'

'I pride myself on being one of the women who've had to sort you out occasionally. . .sir.'

Lucinda, witnessing the harmless banter, decided that Mrs Jackson had thrown in the 'sir' to show that, in spite of her length of service, she still knew her place in the hierarchy.

'What a treasure!' Lucinda observed, as they went out into the cold December night.

'Salt of the earth. . .and she knows it! She's helped me out of a few scrapes in my time.'

She felt his hand under her arm as they reached the bottom of the stone staircase and began to walk across the hospital forecourt.

'Scrapes?' she queried, glancing up at the suave, handsome features above the immaculate pin-stripe suit. 'Somehow I can't imagine you in a scrape. You look as if you were born a consultant.'

His laughter was heartwarming. 'Remind me to show you some of my early photos some time. I think my mother despaired of ever making a doctor out of me. I wanted to be an explorer.'

He was holding open the door of his car, which was almost totally hemmed in between two ambulances. Lucinda climbed in and leaned back against the rich leather upholstery. It was a typical consultant's luxurious limousine, signifying his rank and the affluence of his lifestyle.

'I can't imagine you as an explorer,' she remarked as she fixed her seatbelt.

Jonathan was smiling as he turned on the ignition. She heard the low purring of the powerful engine and her pulses started to race quicker. What had she done to be singled out for the great man's attention so early in her contract at the hospital? Edith Jackson's words came back to taunt her. Seduction or sacking? She could handle either, but she would prefer the former!

Oh, yes! As the car floated effortlessly down along the slushy road that led to the city, she felt she would be a pushover if that was what Jonathan Rathbone had in mind. But it was much too early to consider something like that. She knew that warning bells would ring in her ears if there was any danger of going overboard. She'd made one bad mistake in her emotional life. She wouldn't allow herself to be seduced a second time by a man who simply wanted to make a convenience out of her. Unless there was a firm commitment, she was going to keep her feet planted firmly on the ground. And Jonathan Rathbone would be the last man on earth to offer her a firm commitment!

'So you can't imagine me as an explorer,' he reiterated as he negotiated the car through several lines of traffic to drive past the Tower of London.

'No, you're basically a city man,' she told him, enjoying the warmth of the camaraderie that existed between them. 'A very civilised man who likes comfort and luxury.'

She broke off as her eyes took in the startlingly brilliant scene of the illuminated Tower, covered in a thin blanket of new snow. 'London is such a beautiful city. I think, perhaps, I prefer it after dark when all its imperfections are hidden and only the mysterious outline of the buildings can be seen. Wouldn't you miss London if you moved away?'

'I survived for a while without it, but circumstances forced me back here,' he told her, his eyes steadfastly on the busy road ahead.

'And were you pleased to be back?' she asked.

'No, I wasn't, but. . .oh, it's a long story.'

They were running parallel with the river Thames, the bright lights of the moored boats transforming the snowy scene into a winter wonderland. Lucinda saw that one of the large boats carried a placard advertising Christmas parties on board. 'Still time to book your event,' the flashing neon lights proclaimed.

'How will the ward duties work out over Christmas?' she asked lightly.

He took his eyes briefly from the road. 'Will your boyfriend complain when you tell him you'll be on call?'

She drew in her breath. The only emotion she felt was a deep relief. . .relief that she wouldn't have to consider what to do with a couple of days off at the most vulnerable time of the year. In fact, she had considered volunteering so that the married staff could be with their families.

'No, my boyfriend won't complain,' she replied. 'I shan't even tell him.'

'Won't he want to know? Isn't he interested in what you do?'

Lucinda gave a bitter laugh. 'Not since he married someone else.'

'Ah, I see. But you're obviously still carrying a torch for him.'

'I am not!' she said loudly.

Jonathan laughed and reached across to squeeze her hand. 'Methinks the lady doth protest too much.'

'You can think what you like,' she retorted, when his hand was safely back on the wheel. 'It's been over for five years. I'm now a totally committed career girl, and the freedom is wonderful.'

'It must be,' he observed, as he ploughed through the dense traffic in Parliament Square.

She waited until they were driving along the Embankment again before querying his observation. 'You sound as if you envy my freedom from commitment. Are you married?'

He didn't reply for a few seconds, and she thought that maybe she'd touched on a sore point. When he eventually spoke she thought she detected a huskiness in his voice.

'Not any more.'

She glanced up at the stern profile and didn't know what to make of his reply. But she had the distinct impression that he didn't want to be quizzed any further. And she was trying desperately to check the relief that flooded through her on hearing that he too was a free agent.

He turned off the Embankment and headed towards Chelsea. As the car nosed into a narrow mews and came to a halt in front of a dark mahogany door with a large shiny brass knocker, Lucinda turned to look at him enquiringly.

He switched off the engine and smiled down at her in the half-light.

'I've got to go in and change. Do you want to come in for a drink, or would it compromise your honour to be seen in my bachelor pad?'

She laughed. 'A drink would be fine.' She swung her legs out of the door and stood up on the snow-covered pavement.

Jonathan hurried round the front of the car and put his arm protectively around her shoulder as if trying, in vain, to hold off the snowflakes.

His key ground in the lock and Lucinda felt herself propelled into the warm, dry, luxurious interior. He ushered her into a large, airy drawing-room and pressed a switch that activated numerous concealed lights, several of them hidden in a miniature indoor garden of lush tropical plants. Another switch closed the rich, heavy silk floor-length curtains.

'What would you like to drink?' he asked her.

She settled for a dry martini and leaned back against the soft feather cushions of a large cretonne-covered sofa. From somewhere in the background she could hear the opening strains of Dvořák's Cello Concerto. There was a feeling of unreality about the situation, and she realised she had no idea what their plans for the evening were.

'Where are we going tonight?' she asked, as she sipped her drink.

Jonathan gave her a boyish smile. 'Who said we were going anywhere? I might have simply lured you back to my pad to have my wicked way with you.'

'You might, but then again, I thought you merely

wanted me to report on my day on the ward with Sister Bradwell,' she replied, her tone emulating his playful attitude.

'Was that what I said?' He grinned. 'Now I remember. Well, let's get that out of the way and then we can go out to dinner. I've reserved a table at a little French restaurant just round the corner.' He sprawled himself at the other end of the sofa, seemingly careful not to get too close. 'Now, about that report, Doctor.'

Lucinda took a deep breath before explaining everything that had happened on the ward after he'd left. How the porter had been persuaded to open up the fireplace and eventually get the fire lit. The mothers had loved the innovation. They had even stayed round the fire to have their tea, and the general consensus was that it was a good idea. She was trying not to sound smug.

'Early days,' Jonathan observed drily. 'Give it a month and the porters will be demanding extra pay for the service, the mums will be tired of moving out of their cubicles and the nurses will be screaming for a more orderly routine.'

'I don't think so,' she countered in an even tone.

He laughed. 'We shall see. Well, that's the business finished for the evening. Now we can go out and enjoy ourselves. Give me a few minutes to change.'

She heard him singing above the splashing of the shower in an adjoining room. When he came back into the drawing-room, he seemed to have shed his consultant image with his pin-stripe suit. The casual beige gabardine trousers and dark brown leather jacket made him look years younger. She was glad she hadn't dressed up in anything grand. Her black woollen dress with the single string of pearls that had belonged to her adoptive mother would see her through the evening feeling that she'd got it right.

He was helping her on with her thick camel coat. She found herself taking her time, literally absorbing the feeling of being cosseted. Adrian would never have thought of helping her on with her coat. . .

'You look as if you're miles away,' he said, spinning her round so that she was forced to look up into his dark, searching eyes. 'Penny for them.'

She tried to laugh but failed. 'I was thinking about the past. . .but that's not a good idea.'

He smiled. 'The present is where all the action is. Shall we go?'

She took hold of the arm he offered her. Outside, the snow was thickening.

'We'll leave the car here,' he decided. 'There's nowhere to park outside the restaurant and it's only just round the corner.'

She felt the comforting warmth of his arm around her, holding her gently to his side as they picked their way along the lightly snow-dusted cobbled mews. A waiter held open the door to the restaurant and they ran inside, laughing together as they brushed off the snow.

'Good evening, sir. . .madam. Your usual table is ready for you, sir,' the waiter said, in a deferential voice.

'Thanks, André. You can bring us a couple of very dry martinis.'

Lucinda found herself settled into a chair beside an oak-panelled wall. The dining-room was relatively small, so the atmosphere was cosy but chic. She glanced across at the next table and recognised one of her favourite actresses. A little further along she could see a well-known television presenter. This was obviously the 'in' place, but it looked as if no one cared who was who. It wasn't the sort of restaurant where you simply went to be seen. It looked as if everyone was simply here to enjoy themselves.

She sipped her martini cautiously, so that she could keep her wits about her. Better not relax completely! Not until she'd found out why she'd been invited out.

The menu read like an excerpt from a gourmet cookbook! What should she choose? She looked across at her companion and saw the amused smile on his face.

'Do you like French food?' he asked. 'If not, I can get André to cook you something you really fancy.'

She laughed. 'I adore French food. My mother. . .that is my adoptive mother. . .was French. The only problem with this menu is that I'm spoiled for choice. Let me see. . .' She turned to look up at the waiter and eventually gave him her order.

For the first course, she had ordered langoustine and salmon slices in a shallot vinaigrette.

'Mmm, delicious!' she announced, and smiled

across the table at her host. 'Do you come here often?'

They both laughed at the clichéd line, and Lucinda was relieved to see that all the tension between them had been removed. It was difficult for her to believe that only last week she'd been dreading meeting this man. And now here she was, chatting to him as if she'd known him all her life. . .and rapidly falling for his charm! Oh, well, she decided, this was a special occasion. She didn't know what they were celebrating, but, just for tonight, she was going to throw caution to the wind. It was a long time since she had been out with anyone who'd made her feel like this.

'So your adoptive mother was French, was she? Where did she meet the celebrated Sir James Wilkinson?'

'You've heard of him, then?' She felt a shiver of excitement. Last night her boss and his mother had disclaimed all knowledge of her adoptive father.

'You told me about him, remember?' he replied smoothly. 'You said he was a famous barrister who had been knighted for his philanthropic works. Those were your exact words. So tell me now, where did your adoptive parents meet up?'

'My adoptive mother, Simone, was a lecturer in French at London University. She was forty when she met James. He was nearly sixty and a bachelor. They'd been married a couple of years when they adopted me. I think they'd decided it was too late to have children of their own. At any rate, my mother always used to tell me that I came along just at the right time.'

'You loved her, didn't you?' Jonathan said huskily.

She looked across the table, through the flickering candlelight, and for a moment she couldn't speak. Her heart was too full. Then slowly she drew in her breath.

'Yes, she was very dear to me. . .almost like having a natural mother. I was very sad when she died last year. I felt so alone, without any family. That's when I started to think of trying to contact my real mother. . .'

She broke off and looked across at the tender expression in his eyes. She longed to enlist his help in the search, but he had made it perfectly clear where his allegiance lay.

The waiter was serving exquisitely presented vegetables on to a small dish beside her main course of roast partridge with a lovage sauce. She concentrated once more on the delicious food, unwilling to break up the amicable rapport that had sprung up between them.

Finishing the meal with a simple crème caramel that reminded her of the suppers her adoptive mother had prepared for her, she found herself able at last to believe that her boss had actually asked her out for the pleasure of her company. She took another sip from her wine glass and became even more convinced that he had no ulterior motive.

She smiled across the coffee-cups and tiny chocolates. 'Thank you for inviting me, Jonathan. It's been a lovely evening.'

He reached across the table and lightly touched her hand. 'It's not over yet. Don't talk in the past tense. I thought we might go back to my place.'

She gave a nervous laugh. 'Is this where the seduction scene begins?'

He smiled, and the boyish lines at the side of his deep, expressive eyes creased upwards towards his wide, aristocratic forehead. 'Of course! No, seriously, I do want to talk to you about. . .about a number of matters.'

Warning bells were beginning to ring in her head! 'So you wait until I'm replete with dinner and my brain addled with alcohol,' she observed drily. 'I warn you—I don't mellow as easily as you think.'

Jonathan gave her a wry grin. 'You don't need to mellow. Just listen and agree,' he replied.

She laughed. 'You're pretty sure of yourself, aren't you?'

He stood up and came round to her side of the table. 'You need a certain amount of arrogance to convince people you mean what you say.'

Lucinda looked up into his enigmatic eyes, wondering if he was still joking with her. As she stood up, he took hold of her arm, guiding her through the tables.

'I was only thirty when I took over from my mother,' he continued as he helped her into her coat. 'I was pitched in at the deep end, and no one would have taken me seriously if I'd been pliable.'

She smiled. 'Ah, that accounts for it.'

'Accounts for what?' he asked quickly.

She turned away, willing herself not to say anything she would regret. The waiter was holding open the door, smiling and bowing as they went out into the freezing cold night.

It had stopped snowing, but the existing snow glistened in the lamplight outside the mews doors. They hurried along the slippery cobbles and went into the welcome warmth. As she sank back against the cushions of the sofa, Lucinda began to think about getting back to hospital. Maybe she ought to phone for a taxi. She couldn't expect Jonathan to trek back across London with her. But she'd better hear what it was he had to say to her first.

She could hear him grinding coffee in the kitchen. Presently he appeared with a small tray and poured out a couple of cups of coffee.

She watched him warily from her end of the sofa. He seemed uncharacteristically unsure of himself. Suddenly he put down his cup and faced her.

'I have to be honest with you, Lucinda. It's essential that you stop stirring things up at the hospital. I must have total loyalty from my staff, and your attitude is provocative, to say the least.'

'I knew it was too good to be true,' she breathed harshly. 'What is it you want from me? Total obedience to your every whim? Yes, sir, no, sir, three bags full, sir. . .'

Her tirade was interrupted by the shrilling of a telephone. Saved by the bell! she thought as she watched her boss sprinting across the room. She'd been about to make a complete fool of herself.

Better temper it down a bit. It was such a pity to break up their fragile relationship.

She heard his deep, urgent tone and knew at once it had to be the hospital.

'Yes, we're on our way. Depends on the traffic, but don't worry. Have them set up the theatre. . .'

CHAPTER SIX

As Lucinda looked out of the car she could see the late-night revellers wending their way home through the snow on the Embankment, seemingly without a care in the world. A group of teenagers were having a snowball fight near Cleopatra's Needle and she could hear their youthful, uninhibited laughter. But her own high spirits had sunk as soon as she had heard the nature of the emergency they had to deal with.

And she was still trying to come to terms with the fact that Jonathan Rathbone's interest in her that evening had been inspired by an ulterior motive. She had suspected it all along, but when he had actually put it into words it had come as an unpleasant shock.

She stared out at the unusually white city streets, feeling the misery of knowing she'd been taken for a ride—literally! With all her experience of men she should have known better than allow herself to have romantic daydreams. Still, she was in no worse a position than at the beginning of the evening. Nothing had changed since then. Her opinion of her boss had sunk a little lower, but that was only to be expected. But it mustn't affect her ability to cope with the present medical crisis.

She turned to look at the stern-faced consultant as

he drove through the congested traffic. 'Did they give you a diagnosis?' she asked.

'They wouldn't dare! I prefer to make my own.'

But of course! she thought. Everyone would be waiting for the great man to arrive and take control of the situation.

'Don't you think you ought to delegate?' she said. 'Other hospitals cope without sending for the top man every time there's an emergency.'

'This is not just another emergency,' he countered quietly. 'This is a very dear patient who's been treated for infertility. A month ago I had the pleasure of confirming that she was pregnant. She and her husband were over the moon. They've been trying for a baby for twelve years. And now she's been admitted with acute lower right abdominal pain and vaginal bleeding.'

'I'm sorry,' Lucinda said gently.

'So am I.'

She heard the emotion in his voice and reflected that it was true they were not supposed to become emotionally involved with their patients, but one would have to be a robot not to feel something when dealing with a poignant case like this.

Her boss drove the car furiously into the hospital forecourt, hurtling around a waiting ambulance and screeching to a halt in front of the main door. He jumped out, tossing his car keys towards one of the porters.

'Take care of the car for me, Jim.'

And then he was sprinting off through the main doors and down the corridor. Lucinda followed, assuming that he would want her help. She arrived at the ante-theatre only seconds behind him, trying desperately to catch her breath and regain her composure.

Jonathan was scrubbing up while Sister waited to help him into a sterile gown. A staff nurse came forward and stood in front of Lucinda.

'Can I help you?' she asked unsmilingly.

The consultant turned his head briefly. 'This is my assistant, Dr Barrymore.'

The staff nurse smiled. 'For a moment I didn't know you were one of the staff. I thought. . .'

'Just get on with it, Nurse!' barked the boss.

'Yes, sir!' The staff nurse hurried off to bring another theatre gown.

'Dr Barrymore has a small head,' Jonathan Rathbone called after her.

Lucinda cringed as several pairs of eyes looked down at her over the tops of their masks. She concentrated all her attention on the patient, who was lying on a trolley, partially sedated to ease the pain.

Jonathan Rathbone moved to the patient's side and began his examination. Lucinda watched as the diagnosis she had feared most was confirmed in her own mind.

'There's some tenderness over the gravid tube and in the pouch of Douglas,' he reported quietly. 'And there's peritoneal irritation with some muscle guarding.' He straightened up from the examination and looked at Lucinda. 'What does that suggest to you?'

She glanced at the patient and was relieved to see

that the sedative had taken full effect. 'An ectopic,' she replied instantly.

He nodded gravely. 'We'd better do a laparoscopy to confirm that the pregnancy really is in the Fallopian tube. It seems most likely that we'll have to follow this with a laparotomy to ligate the bleeding points and remove the tube.'

Lucinda glanced at the patient's chart. 'She's already been grouped and cross-matched. Shall I set up the IV?'

He nodded and then turned to look at the theatre sister. 'Everything under control in there, Sister?'

'Of course.'

'Well, let's go, then.'

The laparoscopy did indeed reveal the suspected tubal pregnancy, and Jonathan went ahead with the laparotomy, removing the affected Fallopian tube, while Lucinda ligated the bleeding points. She constantly checked the IV, knowing how essential it was to replace the body fluids the patient had lost in order to improve her general condition. This patient was going to need all her strength to cope with the traumatic sadness she would experience when she learned that the baby she so longed for had been lost.

She looked across the table at her boss as they finished the final sutures. He appeared even more weary than she felt, and she knew that it was more than a physical fatigue. When you were deeply involved with a patient, a disappointment like this could sap your energy level.

He straightened his back and looked around for

Theatre Sister. 'The patient can go back to the ward, Sister. Let me know as soon as she comes round—I want to be the first to explain what's happened.' He turned back to Lucinda. 'Will you take care of the husband for me? He's waiting in reception. I can't face him at the moment, but he's got to be told. The poor chap must be going through hell.'

She nodded as she thought that Jonathan must be feeling really bad to have admitted that there was something he couldn't face. Slowly she turned away from the table and looked around at the team. They were all in the same deflated mood. There was no doubt that the patient's life had been saved, but there was no rejoicing. Only the dreaded knowledge that another poor mother-to-be had been thwarted.

Lucinda walked slowly out of the theatre, pulling off her cap dispiritedly, and throwing it into the nearest bin.

'Why? Why do these things happen?' she muttered as she pushed viciously at the swing doors leading out into the corridor.

'Because your dear friend Mother Nature decides to poke her nose in.'

She looked up, startled, into Jonathan's eyes and realised that he'd hurried forward to hold open the doors for her.

She swung into step beside him as they walked along the deserted corridor. 'Mother Nature didn't sanction the pregnancy in the first place,' she countered. 'Maybe there's a reason why this patient shouldn't become a mother.'

'Perhaps,' he agreed. 'But I think she should be

given the chance. I believe we should use all the technological advances at our disposal. There's nothing quite like the joy of an infertile mother when she holds her test-tube baby for the first time. It's even more joyous than a normal birth, because these women are so desperate to have children.'

'They could always adopt,' she put in, simply to strengthen her argument.

'Not always. You know as well as I do that it's a difficult and complicated business. There's nothing like having your own child.'

'Nature versus nurture,' she murmured. 'The adopted child can be made to feel like a natural child with the right parents. And it can be good for the parents too.'

Jonathan stopped in the middle of the corridor and put his hands on her shoulders, swinging her round to look up into his eyes. 'I'm sorry,' he breathed. 'I didn't mean to touch on a delicate subject. I'm so tired I'd forgotten your own background.'

Lucinda drew in her breath as she saw the unexpected tenderness in his eyes. 'I'm tired too—it's been a long day. So if you'll let me get on with seeing the patient's husband, I'd like to go off duty.'

'I'll come with you,' he said gently. 'It will be easier if there are two of us.'

Relief flooded through her. . .and surprise! She hadn't expected this sudden change of mood. As he released his grip on her shoulders, she fell into step once more.

There was only a dim light in the reception area

and their patient's husband had fallen asleep, lying across three hardback chairs. Lucinda felt a pang of sadness as she saw the relaxed look on the man's face. She glanced down at the notes she was carrying, checking names and dates and the medical history of her patient. She was glad that Jonathan had decided to come with her, because she didn't want to make any embarrassing mistakes at a delicate time like this.

She looked up at her boss. 'Seems a shame to waken him,' she whispered.

He nodded. 'I agree, but the longer we leave it. . .' He put his hand gently on the man's shoulder. 'Mr Morgan. . . Peter. . .'

'How's Kate?' The bewildered husband sat up, rubbing his eyes furiously. 'I must have fallen asleep.'

'Peter, this is my assistant, Dr Barrymore,' Jonathan began quietly. 'I'm afraid we had to operate on Kate. You see. . .'

Lucinda felt herself fighting back the tears as she watched the expression on Peter Morgan's face as he learned the truth. Got to stay calm, she told herself. Must be strong. Even though her legs felt weak with exhaustion she must stay upright and give all the support she could.

When their patient's husband had got over his initial grief they took him along to the staff dining-room. Lucinda went into the kitchen and made a pot of tea. It seemed a pretty useless exercise, but it was the only available comfort besides their own words of sympathy.

After a few minutes they took him along to the ward. He waited in Sister's office until they'd checked on their patient. Kate Morgan had come round from the anaesthetic and was beginning to ask questions.

'I was just about to contact you,' Sister told them as they went towards the patient's bed.

Jonathan nodded. 'You can leave Mrs Morgan to us, Sister.'

Lucinda stood at the bedside, feeling unusually helpless as Jonathan gently broke the bad news. There were no tears, no cries of disappointment. Just a stoic acceptance of another failure.

'The tears will come later,' Jonathan said quietly, as they left the ward where husband and wife were now comforting each other. 'Women like Kate Morgan become so accustomed to failure that they don't allow themselves to believe they'll ever have a child. I've seen some women remain impassive until the baby is actually in their arms, and then they break down and cry for sheer joy.'

'Will that ever happen with Mrs Morgan, do you think? she asked.

'I don't know,' he said wearily. 'Technology can only do so much. We're still reliant on so many extraneous factors.'

'Like wicked old Mother Nature,' Lucinda observed drily.

He gave a short bitter laugh. 'I won't argue with you, for once. It's too late to argue. I'm going to turn in.'

'You're not going home again?'

'Not at this time. I could go to Mother's, but she'd wake up and want to know why I was so late. There's a room in the staff quarters I use on occasions.'

They crossed the forecourt, and Lucinda pulled her coat around her to fend off the freezing cold wind. As she ran up the outside stairs she was deeply aware of Jonathan behind her. Some of her weariness seemed to have disappeared. She decided it must be the bracing night air that was making her pulses race.

'How about a nightcap?' Jonathan asked, as they went into the welcome warmth. 'We ought to round off the social part of our evening that was interrupted.'

She looked up at him warily. 'I have to tell you that I enjoyed the first part of the evening, but if you're planning on starting off where we left off when the phone rang, forget it! I don't want a lecture on your precious hospital routine at this unearthly hour, thank you!'

He smiled. 'That was the last thing I had on my mind, I assure you. We'll have a truce. Let's pretend neither of us is a doctor. We've been out on the town and returned to my place for a glass of my excellent brandy.'

'Now you're talking!' A warning bell was ringing in her ears, but she mentally switched it off. The next few minutes were going to be pure make-believe, as far as she was concerned!

They walked past her door to the far end of the corridor. Jonathan put a key in the lock and pushed open his door. Lucinda went in and looked around, trying to imagine that this room didn't belong to a doctor who just happened to be her boss. It was basically the same room as her own, but looked as if it had been lived in longer than hers. There was an inordinate amount of paper and files lying on the desk. The bookshelves were stacked thickly and had overflowed on to the floor. The general clutter was light years removed from the prestigious pad in Chelsea! She decided this must be where Jonathan did all his work and the mews apartment was where he relaxed.

'Sit down,' he said, throwing a pile of medical journals off the sofa on to the floor. 'The cleaners have despaired of me. They don't venture this far any more.'

She smiled. 'What you need is a good woman. Men are such helpless creatures when it comes to domestic matters. My father used to go to pieces when my mother went away.'

'I nearly went to pieces when I lost my wife,' he said quietly.

She took a sip of her brandy, curling her fingers around the crystal glass, and letting the warm glow relax away some of her tension. She waited for him to elaborate on what had happened, knowing that if she prompted him he might clam up and leave her in suspense.

'It was all so unexpected,' he continued, almost to himself. 'One day she was alive and well, and the next she was dead.'

Lucinda watched as he put down the brandy

decanter and crossed the room with long easy strides to sit down on the sofa. He turned towards her and she saw, with relief, that he looked perfectly in control. He had obviously got over the situation.

'What happened?' she asked gently.

'Victoria was staying with her mother in Scotland while I was at a medical conference in Brussels. She was eight months pregnant and she went into premature labour. Her mother, who was a midwife of the old school, thought she could handle the birth in her own way. She didn't call in the doctor until it was too late. Victoria had a severe postpartum haemorrhage and died in the ambulance on the way to hospital.'

'I'm so sorry,' Lucinda whispered, feeling the inadequacy of her words.

'It should never have happened,' he said in a quiet, controlled voice. 'This is the twentieth century, not the Middle Ages. We've got vast technological resources. . . I'm sorry. . .' He broke off and gave a rueful smile. 'I'm back on my soapbox again! And I promised not to talk shop.'

'I'm glad you told me,' she said gently.

'So am I.' He leaned across and took the brandy glass from her hand.

Her heart was fluttering as the faint scent of his aftershave assailed her nostrils. She was aware of his arms moving to pull her towards him and she remained absolutely still.

'I needed to tell someone just now,' he continued quietly. 'Because tonight, seeing that poor husband, it brought it all back to me.'

Lucinda drew in her breath as she felt the increased pressure of his arms around her. 'You didn't tell me about your baby. Did it. . .?'

'It lived for a few hours. But it was too weak to survive outside an incubator and without expert attention.'

This time she remained silent. There were no words that would soften the blow of such a traumatic experience when they both knew that it should never have happened. She thought of the frustration that he must have suffered, knowing that if only he'd been there his wife and child would have been alive today. It was small wonder he continually preached about the wonders of technology!

She felt a sensual shiver running down her spine as his hands moved around her back, pulling her towards him so that she could feel the beating of his heart against her. For a few moments she remained absolutely still, revelling in the wonderful intimacy of the moment. There was no yesterday, no tomorrow, just that moment when the two of them were in harmony with each other.

Jonathan moved his head so that his lips were close to her own. 'It's wonderful having a truce between us. I wish you weren't a doctor, Lucinda. I wish you were just a woman. . .because. . .'

She felt the unexpected pressure of his lips on hers and she found herself moulding her body against his, wanting to close the gap between them so that she could merge her desire with his. Deep inside her she could feel her dormant senses reeling at the sudden onslaught. Her spine tingled; her whole body was alive with sensuality as she felt his hands caressing her.

Suddenly he broke away and leaned back against the cushions, a boyish smile on his lips as he ran a hand through his dishevelled hair.

'You'd better go before I get too carried away! I didn't mean to trade on your sympathy. It's one thing agreeing to a truce and another trying to seduce you. I'd forgotten who you were.'

She gave him a brittle smile. 'You mean you'd forgotten I was the fly in your hospital ointment.'

'I had indeed.' He leaned forward and put a finger under her chin, lifting it towards his face. 'But a very pretty little fly, if I may say so.'

She pulled away and jumped to her feet. 'Got to go! Goodnight.' The last thing she wanted was for him to start being condescending!

She moved quickly over to the door and waited for him to open it for her.

'I'll walk you to your door,' he told her, but she was already moving away down the corridor, protesting that it wasn't necessary.

She put the key in her own door with trembling fingers, knowing that his eyes were still on her from the other end of the corridor. But she didn't look his way. As she closed the door behind her she leaned against it, breathing heavily, and reflecting that she'd made an awful fool of herself!

CHAPTER SEVEN

LUCINDA had the distinct impression that Jonathan was avoiding her for the next couple of weeks, and that was fine by her! It gave her time to recover some of her injured pride. When she thought of how she had lain in his arms that night after they had performed the salpingectomy she wondered if she needed her head examined! To deliver herself into his hands—literally!—was one of the most stupid things she'd ever done. How was she ever to achieve any of her professional plans if she played around in the enemy camp?

But as she climbed out of bed two days before Christmas she found herself admitting that the sensual experience had been pretty wonderful at the time, and she wouldn't mind repeating it in different circumstances!

She ran into her little shower cubicle and let the water run until it was almost boiling hot. Ouch! It sizzled her skin, but she needed something to bring her to her senses. Because if she spent any more nights dreaming about a certain desirable male she would have to rethink her entire strategy.

She could hear the phone ringing as she wrapped a towel around her wet hair. Yes, she told Sister Bradwell, she'd be along in a few minutes to check on the IV that wasn't functioning properly.

Two minutes with the hair-dryer was all she could afford before throwing a fresh white coat over her clothes, grabbing her stethoscope and heading out into the corridor.

The obstetrics ward was in a somnolent state of early-morning calm before the storm. The new mothers were only half awake as they sipped their tea and waited for their babies to be brought to them. Lucinda hurried to the bed of their latest Caesarian patient and discovered the reason for the malfunction of the IV. Pat Grainger had been a particularly restless patient when they brought her back to the ward, but she had asked not to be given a sedative, saying she would prefer to sleep without medication. Jonathan had strongly advised a sedative, but after he'd gone, Lucinda had readily agreed to her patient's request and forgone the medication.

Now, as she examined the cannula that had been loosened from the patient's arm, she felt a sense of foreboding. Jonathan would be furious!

'You had a bad night, I see, Mrs Grainger,' she observed gently, as she took a new cannula from a sterile pack and prepared to insert it in her patient's arm.

'I was tossing about all night, Doctor. But I was determined to do without a sedative. It's bad enough having to have a Caesarian without adding to it.'

'The Caesarian was unavoidable,' Lucinda told her, as she adjusted the new IV.

'It certainly was! It's the only possible delivery when there's severe placenta praevia.'

Lucinda felt a shiver of apprehension as she heard

Jonathan's voice behind her. 'The IV had packed up,' she began defensively.

'So I see. I presume you decided to ignore my advice and have a natural night's sleep,' he remarked.

The patient smiled. 'We should have listened to you, Dr Rathbone. But I really thought I could manage on my own. Shows how wrong we can be sometimes. I suppose you know what you're talking about.'

Lucinda winced as she fiddled with the IV. She could almost feel the waves of censure flowing out towards her.

Jonathan was smiling down at the patient, his fingers lightly touching her wrist as he felt for her pulse. 'Dr Barrymore leads a crusade to put the clock back to the days when babies were supposed to be delivered from the midwife's bag. She thinks that all technology and medication should be thrown on to the scrapheap. Isn't that so, Dr Barrymore?'

Lucinda moved away from the IV and stood at the bottom of the bed, willing herself to stay calm. A saccharine smile hovered on her lips as she looked up into his sardonic eyes. 'If you say so, sir.'

'It would be so much easier if we could get the stork to bring our babies,' he pursued relentlessly. 'Our mothers could sit beside a mountain stream dabbling their feet while they awaited delivery.'

'Sounds idyllic,' said Lucinda, meeting his gaze without flinching.

'But as it's pure mythology it would be a good idea to remember the concept of pain. Remember pain, Dr Barrymore? That old-fashioned, undesirable four-letter word. . .'

He broke off and looked around the ward, realising that his voice had been too loud. The mothers drifting across the ward towards the newly lit fire were beginning to look his way.

Lucinda found herself stifling a smile. 'You've made your point, Doctor,' she told him. 'I agree with you on this one, so you can get down off your soapbox.'

To her relief she saw him give a boyish grin.

'It's too early in the morning to do battle with you, Lucinda,' he muttered under his breath. 'I wouldn't be quite so magnanimous if I'd been called out to fix that IV myself. Have you had breakfast yet?'

She shook her head.

'That's good, because we're invited over to Mother's, and I thought breakfast would be the least disruptive time. I've got an impossible schedule in the run-down to Christmas.'

'We're invited?' she queried, her heart beginning to pound vigorously.

'Yes, I should have told you days ago. Mother's been asking how you're getting along.' He turned around to look once more at their patient. 'I'll be along later today, Mrs Grainger, to check on that dressing. Try and get some rest. Would you like Sister to give you something to help you relax?'

Pat Grainger nodded sheepishly, deliberately avoiding Lucinda's eyes.

Jonathan scribbled something on the patient's

chart and took it across to Sister Bradwell's desk. 'Fifty milligrammes stat!' he barked, before sweeping out through the swing doors. He paused to hold the door for Lucinda, who was hot on his heels.

'But why breakfast?' she asked, as she almost ran in an attempt to keep up with his long strides.

'I've just told you; I can't make any other time, and Mother wants to see you before Christmas. Can't think why.'

A tremor of excitement passed over her. Could the old lady have decided she was willing to help in the search for information on her mother? Maybe she'd had second thoughts about her uncooperative attitude.

As they went out on to the hospital forecourt a shaft of winter sun burst through the thick clouds. The snow that would have been so welcome on Christmas Day had melted, leaving a treacherous carpet of slush and puddles.

'So much for a white Christmas!' Lucinda said, as she climbed into the passenger seat of Jonathan's car. There was a path across the field behind the X-ray department, but at this time of year it was too muddy to contemplate. The journey by car around the hospital perimeter was longer but infintely more practicable.

'Snow is fine on a Christmas card or a ski-slope, but it can be a dangerous commodity when you're trying to run a hospital,' Jonathan remarked briskly. 'I'm not sorry to see that it's on its way out. It's good to know the roads will soon be clear and the ambulances will have an easier time.'

She looked out of the window as they drove on to the main road. Someone was waving madly to her from the front of the car. She recognised their ectopic patient, Kate Morgan, on her way home, and waved back.

'Was that Kate?' asked Jonathan, his eyes still on the road.

'Yes; her husband arrived at the crack of dawn to take her home. To be honest, I think she would have preferred to spend Christmas in hospital. She hasn't seemed as if she wanted to pick up the threads of her life again, since she lost the baby.'

'That's why it's a good thing she's going home. Besides which, she's not likely to get pregnant again sitting here in hospital like an old woman.'

Lucinda smiled. 'What do you think her chances are?'

He shrugged. 'She's only got one Fallopian tube left. In a few weeks we'll give her another course of fertility treatment.'

'Did she ask for it?'

He shook his head. 'She's still in a state of shock, I think. But her husband came to see me and begged me to put her back on the list. We'll just have to wait and see how she feels about it.'

'She may have decided she's had enough and simply allow nature to take its course,' Lucinda reflected sadly.

'You could be right,' he replied evenly, swinging the car around the gravel drive and pulling it to a halt.

She started to unbutton her white coat, revealing

the warm red woollen dress she'd put on underneath. It was one of the perennials she always brought out at Christmas to put herself in the festive mood. 'Let me leave my coat in the car,' she said. 'I'd prefer to have breakfast in my mufti.'

Jonathan smiled and leaned across to help her out of the white coat. 'As you wish, but I assure you, Mother's used to white coats about the place. You don't have to stand on ceremony. It's only a simple family breakfast.'

But simple it was not! It was as she expected it to be, a veritable banquet, beautifully served at the polished dining-room table. After she'd acquitted herself of half a delicious grapefruit, a bowl of porridge, scrambled eggs and mushrooms, she slowly peeled a ripe pear and sank her teeth into the juicy flesh.

'I like to see a girl with a good appetite,' Dr Mary observed as she looked across the table with a benign smile. 'You remind me of. . .of so many of the young girls who have passed through my hands. In the early days, when the hospital was still mostly for girls in difficult circumstances and their babies, I used to make a point of supervising their food myself. Many of the girls were undernourished, and it was a delight to see them grow stronger under my care.'

Lucinda drew in her breath. 'It's strange to think that you must have cared for my mother.'

The old lady met her questioning gaze without blinking. 'So many girls have passed through my hands,' she murmured in a deadpan voice. 'Would you like some more coffee, my dear?'

'No, thank you.' Lucinda glanced at Jonathan, who had been listening silently to the exchange. 'Will you take me back to the hospital now? I haven't got much time to spare today.'

He stood up. 'That makes two of us.'

Dr Mary put a hand across the table as if to detain Lucinda. 'I do hope you'll call in to see me on Christmas Day,' she said.

Lucinda looked up at Jonathan enquiringly.

'If I can spare Lucinda I'm sure she'll pop in,' he replied briskly. 'But we're going to be very busy. You know what it's like at Christmas, Mother, when you're trying to run the place with a skeleton staff. You only need one emergency to throw a spanner in the works.'

Dr Mary smiled. 'I know. My feet never touched the ground until I retired! But they were the happiest days of my life,' she added wistfully. 'Don't let anyone try to tell you otherwise, my dear,' she told Lucinda. 'And whatever you do, keep working as a doctor after you get married. . .even when the children come along. It's worth it.'

'I'm sure it is,' Lucinda said hastily. 'But, believe me, I haven't any plans in that direction. I'm the original twentieth-century career girl. I don't think I'll ever have time to get married, let alone have any children.'

'Oh, you will, you will,' the old lady nodded sagely. 'You weren't meant to be a lone bird. You'll find your mate soon enough.'

As Lucinda watched Jonathan helping his mother to her feet she had an almost uncontrollable urge to ply her with questions. She felt, instinctively, that Dr Mary remembered her mother perfectly well but was deliberately blocking out the memory. There had to be a reason for this, because the old lady was no fool. Far from it! She was a highly motivated, extremely intelligent woman who had dealt with all sorts of medical problems during her long life as a medical practitioner. And because of this calculated reluctance to impart the information she needed about her mother, Lucinda found herself wondering, albeit grudgingly, whether it wouldn't be better to take the old lady's advice and let sleeping dogs lie.

She walked behind Dr Mary, noting how she leaned heavily against her son's arm but reflecting that she still had all her faculties about her. So if the wise old Dr Mary had decided to keep her in the dark about her mother, maybe she should respect her judgement. If she applied for information through the accepted channels, she might find herself wishing she'd remained in the dark. But she couldn't help thinking that if Dr Mary were to come round to her way of thinking and cushion the blow for her, that would solve the problem. Yes, she could stand any revelation, however dire, if someone who knew the full story were to explain it to her. But how could she persuade Dr Mary to change her mind?

The old lady stood on the front steps as they drove away, smiling and waving her hand. 'You won't forget Christmas Day!' she called after them.

Jonathan pressed the button of his automatic window and called back, 'We won't forget, Mother.'

As the window whirred back to the top he turned briefly to look at Lucinda. 'She never used to be like this,' he told her.

'Like what?'

'Possessive, requiring attention, wanting people to visit her. When I was a child I sometimes didn't see her for days on end.'

'She realises she's getting old and life is slipping by. And she hasn't got her absorbing career any more.'

He shook his head. 'You seem to understand her better than I do. I suppose it's because you're a woman.'

Lucinda smiled. 'No, just a human being.'

He gave a dry laugh. 'And I'm just a machine, I suppose?'

'Sometimes you are. . .hey, aren't we going in the wrong direction? I've got to be back on the wards in. . .'

He changed gear as he pulled into the outside lane of the road leading away from the city. 'Call me a machine if you like, but I still feel the need for some fresh air. Let's play hookey for half an hour and go and feed the ducks in the park.'

She laughed as she watched the stern-faced consultant change into a smiling, relaxed-looking young man.

'I only said you were sometimes like a machine,' she qualified as he turned off the main road and drove up towards Victoria Park. 'And that's nearly always when you're in the hospital. Off duty you can be fun to be with.'

'Please, spare me the exaggerated compliments.' He pulled the car to a halt outside the park and turned to look at her. 'I told you a couple of weeks ago that I wish we didn't have to work together. If only you weren't a doctor, Lucinda!'

She heard the huskiness in his voice and the memory of that passionate encounter in his room came flooding back—not that it had ever been far from her consciousness!

Suddenly he leaned across and kissed her briefly, full on the lips. She felt her pulses racing as she met his tender gaze.

'We must be mad, sitting here in the middle of a working morning,' she began defensively.

Jonathan put his hand under her chin and raised her eyes towards his. 'Don't be so unromantic. I'm supposed to be like a machine, remember?'

'I'm sorry,' she stammered, suddenly confused by the turbulent emotions inside her. Could this exciting man really be the man she loved to hate? 'I feel as you do about the situation between us. I wish we didn't have to work together.'

'But you must admit, we're a pretty good team when we ignore our differences. If only you'd mellow a little, Lucinda.'

She froze as she sensed a lecture on her methods in the offing. 'Let's walk,' she said briskly, pushing open the door of the car. 'I thought we came here for some fresh air.'

His arm under hers was sensually disturbing, but

she found herself enjoying the experience as they made towards the lake. A couple of young mothers with pushchairs and toddlers were throwing crumbs into the water for the noisy ducks. They stood together watching the amusing scene for a couple of minutes.

'I feel as if I'm playing truant from school,' Jonathan whispered in her ear. 'I once did—only once! I never dared to repeat the experience.'

'What happened?' asked Lucinda.

'An outpatient told my mother where I was. She got in her car and drove out here and gave me a lecture on moral responsibility and the importance of sticking to the rules. I've never forgotten how stern and sad she looked at the same time. I was only ten.'

'You poor mite!' Lucinda breathed, and in her mind's eye she could see the little Jonathan standing by the lake, having the last remains of his childhood drummed out of him by a power-crazed career mother.

He gave her a rueful smile. 'Oh, I've always been grateful to my mother for pointing me in the right direction. I needed ticking off. If I were to go my own way, I'd be far too relaxed and nothing would ever get done.'

She laughed. 'I don't believe it. And I really am sorry for calling you a machine.'

He put his arm round her back and squeezed her against his side. 'We've got a lot to learn about each other, you and I, Lucinda.'

'I've got a lot to learn about myself,' she murmured. And then, spurred on by the warmth of feeling between them, she turned and looked up into his eyes. 'Do you think your mother will ever change her mind and fill me in on the details of my background?'

She held her breath as she saw him hesitate. 'She never changes her mind,' he said. 'Make your own enquiries if you must, but leave Mother out of it.'

He turned away, his arm still around her back so that she was forced to move with him. Slowly they made their way back to the car. The dark clouds had massed together and a light drizzle was starting as he held open her door.

The feeling of unreality evaporated as she climbed in. They were returning to the medical world where they had to do battle together—or against each other! She loved her medical work, but at this moment she would have liked to remain out here with Jonathan away from all the pressures of their daily life.

'Penny for them,' he said, hesitating before starting up the engine.

Lucinda smiled. 'I was just having a daydream. Sometimes I wish I weren't a career girl. Sometimes I'd just like to be a person with time to stand and stare.'

'But you are a career girl,' he told her. 'You'll simply have to make time to stand and stare. . .as we did just now. It wasn't the fresh air I needed as much as the company of a delightful female who just happens to bear an uncanny resemblance to an awful ogre of a woman doctor I have to work with.'

'Why, you. . .!'

He caught her in his arms as she launched herself against him. 'Let's have a truce. I must kiss you. . .you look so wonderful when you're angry. . .'

She struggled briefly as his lips sought hers and then the sweet, pleasurable sensations overtook her, making her feel limp, pliable and totally bewildered by this impossibly delectable man. The kiss was brief but earth-shattering! She felt all her resolves going out of the window. She wanted to prostrate herself before this man and agree to his every whim. . .

Steady on! said the rational voice inside her head. Don't let your female hormones seduce you into thinking that you're in love.

But I am in love! screamed her irrational self, struggling to get the better of her. And I don't want to be. . .not with Jonathan Rathbone.

CHAPTER EIGHT

LUCINDA looked out of her bedroom window on Christmas morning and the sight of the winter sun climbing above the rooftops added a glow of happiness to her already excited spirits. She realised that she hadn't felt like this about Christmas for. . .how long was it now. . .five years?

Since Adrian dropped his bombshell, she reminded herself, as she wondered if her high spirits could have anything to do with the way she was feeling about her boss. Who's kidding who? she asked herself as she opened the window and let in a blast of cold air. She knew perfectly well she'd joined Jonathan's long list of admirers! But it was something more than just admiration.

Unconsciously she passed a hand over her lips and experienced again the sensual *frisson* that she'd felt when he had kissed her two days ago beside the park. It had been such an ordinary day, in such an ordinary place, but the situation had been transformed into pure romance for her.

She drew in a couple of deep breaths of fresh air that chilled her, before quickly shutting the window and telling herself there was work to be done even on Christmas morning. . .especially on Christmas morning when half the staff were in the bosom of their families. She couldn't afford the time to start mooning around feeling romantic. And it was high time she tried to forget the romantic side of Dr Jonathan Rathbone and concentrated on reforming some of his stubborn-minded professional ways.

She showered before pulling on her red wool 'Christmas' dress. She had washed it yesterday so that it would be sparkling clean for the festivities today. There were no operations scheduled, so she would probably wear it all day. But she decided, there and then, that next year she would buy something new for Christmas. . .something sexy and slinky and captivating. . .

She broke off with a sigh as she remembered that she didn't know where she would be next Christmas. It was unlikely she would still be working here at the Mary Rathbone. If she managed to accomplish half the reforms she intended, her contract wouldn't be renewed!

If only she could see eye to eye with her boss, she thought as she slung a clean white coat over the dress. He'd told her to mellow, but she had no intention of changing her principles simply to bolster his professional ego. Determinedly, she reached for her stethoscope before hurrying out into the corridor.

'Steady on!'

She looked up in embarrassment when she heard Jonathan's voice and felt his strong arms steadying her as she almost collided with him outside her door.

'I'm sorry,' she blurted out, embarrassed by the slow blush that had started to sweep over her face.

'Happy Christmas, Doctor,' Jonathan said, an amused smile on his tantalisingly handsome face.

'Happy Christmas!' she returned, and made to move away.

'I was about to have breakfast. Care to join me?'

'Why not?' She fell into step with him.

Together they negotiated the outside staircase to the forecourt. The ambulances were standing silent and inactive and there were very few cars parked in front of the hospital.

'Everything's quiet; let's hope it stays that way,' Jonathan said, as he accompanied her through the swing doors and along the corridor to the dining-room.

Lucinda nodded in agreement. 'I can't think of any reason why we shouldn't have a peaceful day,' she observed, as they sat down at one of the holly-bedecked tables. 'We've discharged masses of patients this week and the remaining ones shouldn't present any problems.'

He laughed, and the sound of his laughter sent a sensual shiver down her spine.

'Don't speak too soon, and don't make idle predictions, my girl! You should know better than that. When you've had as many Christmases in hospital as I have you'll know that anything can happen. . .and often does!'

She picked up her coffee-cup and drank deeply. 'I've had a number of Christmases in hospital,' she said quietly as she put down her cup. 'I've always made a point of volunteering to be on duty. Hospitals are such happy places at Christmas, and it means you can forget your own problems.'

She stopped and looked across the table to where Jonathan was absentmindedly buttering a piece of toast. 'You don't have to tell me,' he said softly. 'I've spent every Christmas on duty since Victoria died.'

She gave him a gentle smile. 'Adrian and I planned to marry five Christmases ago. I'd bought a long-sleeved ivory satin dress with a high mandarin collar so that I wouldn't be too cold in the village church. My father. . .my adoptive father, that is. . .was going to perform the ceremony. . .' Her voice began to fade away as she became aware of his rapt attention.

'Go on,' he urged gently. 'I'd like to hear what happened.'

Lucinda took a deep breath as she looked around the almost deserted dining-room. At times like this is was good to have a sympathetic ear. . .and Jonathan had such empathy with her when he wasn't playing the arrogant boss.

'My father developed a malignant tumour of the brain. He went into hospital on the day that Adrian broke off our engagement,' she told him.

Jonathan reached across and took hold of her hand. She remained motionless, enjoying the comforting feel of his fingers around hers.

'So Christmas was an unhappy time that year,' he prompted, in a sympathetic voice.

She gave a bleak smile. 'Yes, you could say that. My father died on Christmas Eve. . .but this will never do!' She pulled away her hand and tried to put some warmth into her smile. 'I'm sorry. . . I didn't mean to depress you. It's all in the past now and. . .'

'You didn't depress me,' he told her quietly. 'Traumatic periods are best shared with someone. I think you've been unconsciously hiding away your problems. It's best to get them out into the open.'

Lucinda reached for a croissant, freshly baked that morning in the hospital kitchen. 'It certainly is best to get things off your chest. You may be right, Jonathan. I've tried to blot out all my thoughts of what happened five years ago. I'd like to get on with living in the present.'

'We could make this one of your happiest Christmases,' he said, his eyes alight with tenderness. 'Would you have supper with me tonight? I plan to go back to the apartment and celebrate.'

She drew in her breath as she tried to calm her beating heart. Things were moving too fast! Was she ready for the sort of special relationship that was building up between them? Could she handle the professional and private implications?

Yes, of course you can! said the romantic side of her. Immediately, the voice of reason told her to tread carefully and not to surrender the cherished individuality she had struggled so long to preserve.

She tried hard to look cool and collected as she nodded her head, making a calculated compromise. 'It's rather a long way across town to go for supper at the end of today. Maybe we could have something nearer the hospital.'

Jonathan laughed. 'You think I'm luring you back to my pad with nefarious intentions, don't you?'

She gave him a wry smile. 'I can handle myself. I'm not a child. Nor do I fancy trekking back in the small hours of the morning.'

'You could always stay the night. . .in my spare room,' he added with a calculatedly wicked grin.

Her pulses were racing. 'I'll let you know,' she said calmly, standing up to hide her confusion.

He rose to his feet. 'Let's do some work,' he said.

As they walked along the corridor together, Lucinda was trying desperately to regain her composure. The more she saw of Jonathan in an off-duty situation the more she was attracted to him. . .no, more than that. . .the more she was falling in love with him. But how did you work with a man whom you regarded as two separate beings? There was the stern doctor who had so often opposed her ideas and the wonderful, romantic, sensually disturbing. . .

Steady on! she told herself as she ducked under the arm that was holding open the door to the obstetrics ward. Don't go overboard for him. . .well, at least, not until tonight!

There were only four mothers sitting feeding their babies around the fireplace that morning. Lucinda and Jonathan joined the happy group and chatted with them about how the babies were getting on. There were no obvious problems and the general air of holiday and relaxation made their work seem like pure pleasure. One of the mothers began to recount an amusing story of her own childhood that brought a smile to everybody's lips.

It was at this point that the ward door opened and Lucinda saw the dour figure of Dr Mary striding purposefully in. The old lady stopped in her tracks as she regarded the intimate little group gathered around the burning fire.

'Whose idea was this?' she asked, in a quavering voice.

An unnatural silence settled on the ward. The mothers looked from one to the other with perplexed expressions. Lucinda was the first to break the silence. She stood up at the same time as Jonathan marched across the room to take his mother by the arm and escort her towards the fireplace.

'Sit next to the fire, Dr Mary,' Lucinda said, with a calmness she didn't feel. 'It was my idea that the mothers should feed their babies in a more relaxed situation.'

'Of course it was your idea. It had to be,' the old doctor muttered in a harsh tone.

Lucinda sat down again and turned to look at Dr Mary, but what she saw disturbed her more than the anger she fully expected. There were tears in the old lady's eyes and the wrinkled frown on her face was quivering as if an attempt was being made to stem the flow.

The old lady put out a gnarled hand and touched her lightly on the cheek. 'How did you know?'

Lucinda stared at her, perplexed. 'Know what?'

'That this was how it used to be. . .the winter you were born.'

Lucinda felt a creeping sensation over her skin. So she did remember, after all!

Jonathan moved behind his mother's chair and

put a restraining hand on her shoulder. 'Mother, I don't think you. . .'

'It was so cold we had to keep the fire burning night and day. . .' The old lady broke off and looked around her as if suddenly remembering that she wasn't alone.

Lucinda held her breath. For a few moments, Dr Mary had looked as if she was reliving the past. 'Tell me about it,' she urged.

Dr Mary frowned and her voice had regained its normality when she spoke in an authoritative tone. 'I don't remember anything except that the winter was very cold. The next year we got central heating and I had the fireplaces boarded up.'

'But how did you know it was the year I was born?' Lucinda persisted earnestly. Dr Mary had opened the can of worms; there was no reason why she should slam the lid back on.

The old lady's eyes held a guarded, veiled expression. 'It may have been. . .or it may not. I know how old you are, Dr Barrymore, but my memory of those days is very hazy. . . Now, I came to wish you all a happy Christmas!' She beamed around at the mothers, who had been intently listening to the conversation. 'My cook has made you all some mince pies to have with your mid-morning hot drink.'

Lucinda, listening to the polite murmurs of thanks, thought that the scenario resembled a royal visit. Dr Mary sat among them like the queen of the establishment, which she undoubtedly still was. If the old lady was regretting her momentary lapse into reminiscence, she made no sign of it. Oh yes, it was true that she had the ability to forget unpleasant memories. Was that what she was deliberately doing now?

The mothers were drifting back to their beds, carrying their precious babies. Lucinda stood up and moved away from the fire, saying that she wanted to examine her Caesarian patient's abdomen.

'Lucinda,' Dr Mary said quietly.

Lucinda turned back and summoned every effort to fix a polite smile on her face.

'I hope you will be able to come and have Christmas dinner with me. I shall be waiting at two o'clock.'

'I'm not sure,' Lucinda began. 'We have to carve the turkeys and serve the patients. I doubt if. . .'

'Oh, I know all about that,' interrupted the old lady with a disparaging wave of her hand. 'What do you think I did all those years ago? There'll be plenty of time when the patients are settled back on their pillows with their paper hats and crackers.' She turned to look at her son. 'Jonathan, I shall expect you both. Don't be late, because I want to hear the Queen's speech at three o'clock.'

'We'll do our best. Now if you'll excuse me I've got work to do, Mother.'

The old lady frowned. 'Oh, but I thought you'd escort me around the hospital. I'd like to wish everyone a happy Christmas. And I need to talk to you,' she added in a quiet voice.

Jonathan glanced across at Lucinda, who had

already reached her patient's bedside. 'Can you cope in here alone, Dr Barrymore?' he asked.

Lucinda smiled. 'Of course; why ever not?' She pulled the curtains around Pat Grainger's bed and felt relieved to avoid Dr Mary's searching eyes. How long would the old lady go on tantalising her like this with her hints and half truths? It was almost as if she enjoyed keeping her in suspense.

She heard Jonathan and his mother leaving the ward as she prepared her patient for examination. Sister Bradwell came rustling in through the curtains with an examination trolley.

'Sorry to keep you, Doctor. I couldn't get away from Dr Mary. She's in one of her talkative moods.'

Lucinda bent over her patient and removed the dressing with sterile forceps. She concentrated all her attention on checking the surrounding area, carefully palpating the abdomen until she had satisfied herself that all was well.

'First class!' she announced as she straightened up and smiled down at her patient. 'You'll be good as new in a few days.'

Pat Grainger smiled happily. 'Thanks, Doctor. You've all been great. I feel so sorry for you, having to work on Christmas Day.'

Lucinda laughed. 'Some of us actually like it, you know.'

'But haven't you got a family waiting for you at home?' Mrs Grainger persisted.

'No, actually I haven't,' Lucinda replied calmly as she peeled off her surgical gloves and tossed them into a kidney dish.

'I was listening to what old Dr Mary was saying,' the patient continued eagerly. 'Were you born here in this hospital. . .maybe even in this very ward?'

Lucinda felt a lump rising in her throat. 'Perhaps,' she answered, with a steady smile on her lips.

Sister Bradwell was busying herself with the trolley before pulling back the curtains. 'Coffee, Doctor?' she asked briskly.

'Lovely!' Lucinda turned back to say goodbye to her patient with a feeling of relief.

Cynthia Bradwell's office was an oasis of calm. Lucinda sank down into one of the comfortable old armchairs and accepted the coffee cup that was held out towards her.

'Happy Christmas!' the sister said to her. 'I hope the old lady didn't spoil it for you.'

Lucinda smiled. 'No, of course not. I just wish she wouldn't throw out little snippets of information and then clam up again.'

'How much do you actually know?' Sister Bradwell asked in a cautious voice.

'I was born here. . .in this hospital. There's no doubt about that. But I don't know the name of my natural mother or my father.'

'But why don't you check it out with the registrar of births?'

'I would prefer to have the information volunteered to me, because the more insinuations that are made, the more apprehensive I feel.' Lucinda gave a wry grin. 'Perhaps that doesn't make sense to you, but when you're personally involved. . .'

'I can see what you mean,' Sister Bradwell put in

hastily. 'If something unpleasant has happened you'd like to know the truth at first hand.'

Lucinda smiled. 'Exactly! And I have the awful feeling that Dr Mary is holding something back.'

'Why don't you have a word with the medical secretary over in the staff quarters. . .you know, Edith Jackson. She's been here for about thirty years, to my knowledge. I've always found her very helpful. Failing that, you could try Dr Mary's old housekeeper, Hilda Banks. Rumour has it she was an absolute tartar of a theatre sister, but she's mellowed in her old age. You might be able to worm something out of her if you try.'

Lucinda gave a brittle laugh. 'I think I'll try Edith Jackson first. She seems the more approachable of the two. Old Mrs Banks is a good housekeeper, but you don't feel at ease when she's around the place, do you?'

'I wouldn't know,' Cynthia Bradwell replied. 'I've never been invited across to the royal palace. Very few people have, so you're honoured. I think Dr Mary must like you, in spite of being such a cussed old so-and-so with you. Or is it Dr Jonathan who's twisting her arm into accepting you?'

'Neither,' Lucinda replied lightly. 'My visits are purely professional. Dr Mary needs to be reassured that the hospital is still running smoothly.' She put her cup down beside a well-thumbed pile of nursing magazines and stood up. 'I must get on, or I'll never be finished in time to carve the turkey on Children's Surgical. Apparently all our names were put into a hat. I hope they won't be disappointed it's me. I've only got a couple of patients on that ward.'

'Jonathan is going to carve ours,' Cynthia Bradwell said in a bland tone. 'I think somebody must have fixed that one. The mothers would have gone on strike if he hadn't shown up. They adore him.'

Lucinda gave an easy smile. 'I know. . .and so does he, by the way he lords it over them. Can't put a foot wrong, can he?'

Sister Bradwell laughed. 'Not with me, he can't. I've joined his fan club. How about you, Doctor?'

'Ah, that would be telling,' Lucinda replied with a guarded smile.

CHAPTER NINE

LUCINDA spent the rest of the morning checking on all her patients in the various wards before hurrying over to the staff quarters in search of Edith Jackson. Strike while the iron's hot, she told herself. No more procrastination! There would just be time to see the medical secretary before returning to hospital to carve the turkey in Children's Surgical.

Mrs Jackson looked up from her desk as Lucinda approached. 'What can I do for you, Dr Barrymore?' she asked.

Lucinda was encouraged by the beaming smile on the older lady's kindly face. 'I've only got a few minutes to spare,' she began breathlessly. 'You may think it's an odd request, coming on Christmas Day, but there are so many memories flooding back. Everybody's getting sentimental and nostalgic. . .you know how it is. . .'

'Oh yes, indeed. I can remember all my Christmases. . .'

'You can? Do you remember twenty-eight years ago? That's how old I'll be in January, and I was born in this hospital. So my mother must have been attending the ante-natal clinic at the time. . .and then she would have been admitted in January. I was adopted soon after birth. . . I'm afraid I don't know my mother's name, but. . .'

'Well, I'm blessed!' exclaimed Mrs Jackson. 'You are a dark horse! And you really don't know your mother's name?'

Lucinda gave a nervous smile. 'My adoptive parents always insisted that it wasn't necessary for me to know who she was. But they're both dead now, so I'd like to find out something about her.'

'Well, why don't we go and have a look in the Records Department? There'll be nobody there today, but I've got the keys. It would be like a Christmas present if we found out what you were looking for, wouldn't it?'

'Are you sure it's OK to look through the records?' Lucinda asked, feeling suddenly apprehensive.

'You've got a right to know, Dr Barrymore,' Mrs Jackson replied, heaving her ample body from the swivel chair. 'And I must admit I'm intrigued myself. As soon as we find out the name I'm sure I'll be able to put a face to it. It's funny, you know, I can remember some of our mothers from way back as if it was yesterday. Photographic memory, some people would call it. . .'

The incessant flow of words did nothing to soothe Lucinda's nerves. Was she actually about to discover the truth? Was it really this easy? She walked beside the secretary down the steps and across to the hospital. The chill wind blew through her white coat and penetrated the woollen dress. She shivered. . .but she knew it wasn't just the cold!

Edith Jackson unlocked the door and marched

into the Records Department. 'Now, give me a few preliminary details. . .date of birth. . .'

Lucinda's voice cracked as she filled the secretary in with the relevant information.

Mrs Jackson nodded as she started on one of the filing cabinets. 'All the modern records are now on computer, but we haven't bothered to transfer the really old cases. . .not that twenty-eight is old, but you know what I mean, Doctor,' she added with a sympathetic smile.

Lucinda attempted to smile back. Yes, she knew what Mrs Jackson meant. She only wished the secretary would stem the endless chatter. She meant well, but. . .

'January the second, you said, didn't you? Yes, here it is. . .'

There was an ominous pause. Having hated the chatter Lucinda now felt herself thrown off guard.

'Well, what have you found?' she blurted out.

Mrs Jackson turned to look at her. 'You're little Vanessa's daughter,' she said in a barely audible voice.

Neither of them had heard the door opening, but now the secretary stared behind Lucinda with a frightened look. Lucinda turned to find Jonathan and his mother standing in the doorway.

'What do you think you're doing, Edith?' Dr Mary asked in an icy voice.

'I was helping Dr Barrymore, Dr Mary.' The secretary twisted her hands nervously. 'I'd no idea she was Vanessa's daughter. If I'd known I would never. . .'

'That's enough, Edith. You'd better go back to your desk.' The old lady's face was twisted with anger as she glared at Mrs Jackson. When she turned to face Lucinda some of the facial lines softened. She waited until the secretary had gone out before speaking again.

'I asked you not to continue your search here at the hospital, Lucinda. I advised you to go through the official channels.'

Lucinda ignored the criticism. 'Tell me about Vanessa, Dr Mary. Tell me about my mother.'

The old lady turned away. 'Not now, child. You have to go to the wards and ensure that the patients have a happy Christmas. Afterwards, when you come to lunch, I'll tell you something about Vanessa.' She looked up at Jonathan, who had been standing tight-lipped beside her. 'Make sure everything is securely locked up in this department.'

Lucinda took a deep breath as she tried to calm her feelings of frustration. To be so near the truth. . .so near and yet so far! Could she trust Dr Mary to keep her promise, or would she decide to play the senile old lady with a conveniently forgetful memory again?

'I'm going to Children's Surgical,' Lucinda said briskly, as she walked out through the door, not trusting herself to make any further comment on the unnerving situation.

The young patients were waiting for her when she arrived at the ward. Somehow she managed to smile and joke with them, even laughing occasionally at the antics of the ambulant patients, but her mind was preoccupied. She donned her chef's hat and carved the turkey as if she were performing a difficult surgical operation. The nurses and patients hooted with laughter as she insisted that Sister hand over the carving knife with a gloved hand as if it were a scalpel.

When the make-believe operation had been performed she handed out plates of turkey and vegetables for the excited youngsters, and later poured custard sauce over the Christmas pudding. There were crackers to be pulled and balloons to be blown, and she entered into the spirit of the occasion, but deep down inside she was apprehensive, longing for the time to come when she would be able to go across to see Dr Mary, but dreading what might be revealed.

It was nearly two o'clock when Jonathan popped his head round the ward door. Sister hurried forward to meet him, urging him to join in the fun, but he declined with a smile.

'Sorry I can't stay, Sister. I just called in to see if Dr Barrymore was still here.'

Lucinda felt the colour rising to her cheeks as she said her goodbyes and made her way to the ward door. A couple of children were still clinging to her hands, and she had to promise to return again soon as she handed them over to the care of the nurses.

The doors closed behind them and Jonathan put an arm under hers. 'Mustn't be late or we'll both be in the doghouse.'

'I think I've blotted my copybook forever as far as

your mother is concerned,' she said as they hurried towards the main door.

'I don't think so,' he told her, nodding to the porter who opened the door for them. 'My lord, it's cold out here!' His arm under hers urged her to run towards his car.

Breathless and cold, she turned towards him when she was seated in the passenger seat. 'Why don't you think so?' she asked.

'I'm not sure,' he replied in a guarded tone, as he started up the engine. 'I know her better than you do, and she seems unnaturally tolerant at the moment. Besides which, I think she knows, deep down, that you had a perfect right to the information.'

'But I only know my mother's name! Vanessa . . .that's not information,' Lucinda protested heatedly.

'She's promised to tell you more,' he replied. 'So prepare yourself. The reason she's been holding back is that she thought it was in your best interests not to know.'

'Is that what she told you?'

'Yes; the first time you broached the subject. . .you remember that evening when you came over? Well, when I escorted her to her room, she told me that she only had your best interests at heart. She told me to discourage you from making enquiries.'

'But why?' Lucinda persisted.

'That's what we're going to find out. Believe me,

Lucinda, I want to learn the truth as much as you do. I'm as much in the dark as you are.'

She was silent until they reached the house. As Jonathan turned off the engine he put a hand across and squeezed her fingers. 'Nervous?' he asked.

The tension that had been building up inside her seemed to evaporate as she looked across into his eyes. The expression of tenderness she saw was deeply comforting. Suddenly she knew she could face anything with this man by her side.

'No, I'm not nervous,' she replied, 'I simply want to know the truth. . .however unpleasant it might be.'

He flashed her a broad, encouraging smile. 'Come on, then!'

Dr Mary was waiting for them in the drawing-room, a silver tray set with crystal glasses and a decanter of sherry beside her on the small, antique side-table.

'I'm glad you could make it, my dear.' She smiled at Lucinda. 'Do sit down. Jonathan will pour us all a glass of sherry.'

Lucinda sat on the edge of the high-backed velvet chair as she sipped her sherry and made polite conversation. She was wondering how long it would be before Dr Mary broached the subject nearest to her heart. It would be foolish to jump the gun and upset the old lady again.

Mrs Banks came in after a few minutes to announce that the Christmas dinner was ready to be served. Lucinda stood up, without waiting to be asked, and began to move towards the door. The sooner they got on with the meal, the more mellow the old lady was likely to get!

Jonathan took his mother's arm, so Lucinda was obliged to follow behind along the corridor to the dining-room. The table looked festive and inviting with a centre bowl of Christmas roses and red linen napkins instead of the white, stiffly starched ones that usually graced the table. There was a holly wreath over the fireplace where a log fire crackled with seasonal charm.

Jonathan held out a chair for Lucinda to take her place on his left hand. As he sat down at the head of the table he turned to look at his mother and complimented her on the appearance of the dining-room. 'I've never seen it look like this since I was a child.'

'I asked Hilda to make a special effort this year, because of our guest.' The old lady smiled across at Lucinda.

Lucinda smiled back. 'You're very kind,' she said in a polite voice.

There were crackers to be pulled before Jonathan stood up and carved the turkey with as much panache as he exercised in theatre.

'It's a pity your students can't see you now,' Lucinda remarked, with a playful smile. She took a sip of the excellent claret that Jonathan had poured for her. Better not drink too much of this, she reminded herself. Got to keep a clear head. . .and not only for her return to duty later in the evening!

When the traditional turkey course had been cleared away, Mrs Banks came in carrying the pudding, flaming in brandy. Lucinda had to say no to the mince pies at the end of the meal, but she accepted a thin chocolate mint with her coffee as they settled themselves back in the drawing-room.

How much longer? she was thinking. Throughout the meal, Dr Mary had steered the conversation around every topic except the required one. They had discussed the West End theatres, the concerts at the Barbican and the Festival Hall, whether there was a future for the cinema now that everyone spent so much time watching television. If Dr Mary didn't say something soon, Lucinda planned to lead the way and to hell with the consequences!

'Now, my dear, about your little discovery in Records this morning.'

Dr Mary's quiet voice cut in on Lucinda's thoughts. She braced herself, put down her coffee-cup and faced the old lady with a pseudo-confident smile.

'I'm glad you've decided to tell me the truth about my mother,' she said evenly.

'Ah, now—come, come, you've rather forced my hand. As you know, I felt it was in your own best interest that you shouldn't know about your mother. You've had a good life so far, with loving and affluent parents who were able to give you a good education so that. . .'

'Dr Mary, stop reminding me of the advantages I've had! I'm very grateful to my adoptive parents, but I felt so alone in the world when they died. Tell me about Vanessa. . . Mrs Jackson remembered her; she said I was little Vanessa's daughter and. . .'

Lucinda broke off with dismay as once again she saw tears in Dr Mary's eyes.

'You won't like the truth, but you force me to give it to you.' Dr Mary took a deep breath. 'Your mother was an orphan. She had no family of her own. She was only sixteen and unmarried when you were born. She died a few days later. . . I forget the exact date, but it will be in the records.'

Lucinda remained absolutely still. She felt in a state of shock. She had hoped against hope that she would get to meet her mother. She'd realised that there must be some awful secret about her, but she had thought that maybe her mother would have some kind of physical or mental disability. But at least she would have been able to meet her. A deep feeling of desolation swept over her. She was still alone in the world. She still had no family. . .but she had a wonderful future in front of her, and life was very good at the moment.

She stood up and walked over to the window, looking out across the large grounds towards the high wall that shielded them from the busy main road.

'I'm glad you told me the truth,' she said quietly. 'I can stop wondering now. I'm on my own again, and it doesn't worry me.' She turned to face Dr Mary. 'But please tell me, how did my mother die?'

Dr Mary frowned. 'She died of pneumonia,' was the barely audible reply.

'Pneumonia? Here in the hospital? Was she suffering from pneumonia when she was admitted?'

'Questions, questions! I can't remember any more

about the case. We don't keep detailed records for more than twenty years. If you search through everything we have on your mother it will only say that she died of pneumonia. And that's what was written on her death certificate, should you decide to apply for a copy.'

Lucinda took a deep breath. 'How did my father take her death? I know you said she was unmarried, but presumably. . .'

'If you'd applied for a copy of your birth certificate you would have found that your father is unknown.' Dr Mary was struggling to her feet, a look of intense weariness on her face. 'Help me to my room, Jonathan. I need to rest. Christmas is such an exhausting time.'

Lucinda remained by the window, tears pricking behind her eyelids as she watched Jonathan escorting his mother from the room. When they had gone she turned back to look out at the wintry scene. She felt as if she'd been slapped in the face for a second time. To have a mother who had died soon after she was born was bad enough, but to have a father who didn't want to know. . . Maybe he wasn't even aware of her existence. . .that would be even worse, because it would imply that her mother was. . .she couldn't bring herself to pronounce judgement on the sixteen-year-old Vanessa.

She stiffened as she heard Jonathan's footsteps returning. He came up behind her and put his hands on her shoulders. 'I'm sorry,' he said quietly.

She turned and his arms went around her, folding her in an embrace that was at once comforting and at the same time disturbing. She looked up into his eyes, sensually disturbed by the very nearness of him. He bent his head and kissed her gently on the lips. She tried not to respond, but emotions deep inside her were forced to the surface. She could trust this man. . .he wouldn't let her down.

She revelled in the sensation of his long, sensitive fingers caressing her spine and found herself wishing she hadn't worn such a thick woollen dress. What she really would like was to feel those fingers against her bare skin so that she didn't miss the slightest nuance of sensual pleasure. . .

Suddenly Jonathan broke away from her. 'Why don't we drive over to my place? It's more relaxing than here. Any minute now, Mrs Banks will come barging in.'

Lucinda smiled. 'Who's going to run the hospital?'

'We'll call in and see if everything's running smoothly. They've got enough staff to cope and I can tell them where I am if they need me. It only takes a few minutes to drive back along the Embankment when there's no traffic.' He put a finger under her chin and stared down into her eyes as if trying to find out what she was thinking. 'You've had an awful shock, Lucinda. It will do you good to get away for a while and relax.'

She gave a short, dry laugh. 'Ah, so you're speaking as my own personal physician, is that it?'

He gave a broad smile. 'Something like that. . .or perhaps I just want to be alone with you in an off-duty situation. No white coats, no stethoscopes, no hurried consultations about surgical procedure. . .just you and I. . .and maybe a wicked bottle of champagne.'

'Which we'll drink sitting out on your balcony in the moonlight,' she mimicked, smiling, as she entered into the spirit of the occasion. 'And we'll look out across the iridescent river to. . .'

He was grinning as he interrupted her. 'Now that would be a bit more difficult, because there are a few tall houses between my place and the river, and if I open the balcony door the wind would probably tear the place apart. But the main thing is that you've agreed to drive over there with me.'

'Have I?'

He bent down and kissed her briefly on the lips. 'You haven't said the words, but you know that's what you want.'

They were strangely silent as they drove back to the hospital, each of them seemingly wrapped up in their own thoughts. They parted at the main door, agreeing to meet up as soon as they'd done a round of the hospital, splitting the departments between them.

Lucinda found the festivities were in full swing everywhere she went. It was difficult to decline all the invitations to join in the fun, and she made a point of spending some time on Children's Surgical, as she had promised. But she was pleased to see that everything was under control. Some off-duty staff had returned, so there was no reason why she and Jonathan shouldn't escape for a while.

Escape! That was the word that sprang to her

mind when she thought of driving off with Jonathan. It was going to be pure escapism. They both needed time to themselves away from the pressures of the hospital, away from the medical problems that so often divided them. For a short time at the end of this memorable Christmas Day she would allow herself to be just a woman. And she would forget the medical side of Dr Jonathan Rathbone. Tonight, he was merely a man. . .and a very desirable one.

CHAPTER TEN

THE Thames Embankment was practically deserted as they drove westwards. A thin drizzle of rain was pattering on the windscreen, but it did nothing to dampen Lucinda's feeling of excitement. For the first time in five years she felt totally free. There had been a shadow hanging over her since she had started speculating about her mother, but now that she had actually been confronted with the truth—unpleasant as it was—she could begin to live her own life again. She told herself that there was nothing she could do about her unfortunate ancestry, so it was best to try to put it out of her mind and concentrate on the present. . .and the future. Could there really be a future for her with this wonderful man?

She looked across at him in the half-light as they waited at traffic lights. He must have sensed her scrutiny, because he turned and gave her a smile that sent her pulses racing. He put out a hand and covered her own.

'You're not regretting coming out with me, are you?'

She smiled. 'Of course not.'

She tried to convince herself that she hadn't made a momentous decision, as she watched Jonathan turning his attention back to the road. She was merely going over to celebrate the end of Christmas Day with a rather special friend.

She looked out across the Thames at the lights of the Festival Hall. Somewhere in the papers she'd read that they were holding a Christmas Day carol concert. A large pleasure boat was passing under Hungerford Bridge, its lights illuminating the mysterious, dark, swirling waters of the river. Everyone was entitled to celebrate Christmas in their own way, and that was just what she was going to do.

But as she turned back to look at the wet road she knew that she had made a decision. . .to let herself fall in love with Jonathan, the man. . .and deal with the vagaries of Dr Rathbone, the consultant, some time in the future. What was it the Spaniards said when they wanted to put something off? She smiled to herself as she said the word out loud, '*Mañana*.'

'*Mañana*?' Jonathan repeated, his eyes still on the road. 'What's so special about tomorrow?'

Lucinda stirred against the back of her seat. 'It never comes.'

He laughed. 'I think you've flipped.'

'Maybe I have,' she said softly.

Jonathan's apartment seemed warm and cosy in contrast to the bleak outdoor scene. As he helped her out of her coat the touch of his fingers on her shoulders started up a train of sensations deep inside her. She no longer had any illusions about what she wanted tonight.

Jonathan disappeared into the kitchen and returned with a bottle of champagne.

While he was away Lucinda amused herself pressing the various switches. The curtains swished along, blocking out the wintry night, while the concealed lighting cast a romantic glow over the elegant drawing-room.

'I've checked the temperature on the balcony,' she told him, smiling. 'And you were right—it's pretty arctic out there.'

He was laughing boyishly as he sank down on to the sofa beside her, balancing the champagne bottle in one hand and a couple of long-stemmed glasses in the other. 'Then we'll have to make do with an indoor celebration. Hold this glass.'

She watched him working on the cork and held out her glass in anticipation. The champagne flowed out in an effervescent surge that seemed to mirror her deliberately carefree mood.

He held his glass towards hers. As the crystal touched he looked directly into her eyes. 'To us!'

She echoed his toast, revelling in her mounting excitement as she took her first sip.

He reached across to the console on the side-table to select some music. Seconds later the room was filled with the haunting strains of Mendelssohn's Violin Concerto.

Lucinda watched as he leaned back against the soft cushions, a look of deep satisfaction on his face.

'I love the music of the Romantic era,' he murmured. 'How about you?'

She put down her glass and eased herself to the back of the sofa. The enormous width of the seat cushions forced her to lift her short legs up underneath her. She found it was quite impossible for her feet to reach the ground.

'The Romantic era is my favourite too, not just for music. I think the artists of the period. . .'

She got no further, because he leaned across and pressed his lips against hers. Oh, the blissful sensations that were sweeping over her! He pulled her closer and she snuggled against him, loving the distinctive odour of the after-shave on his vigorous male body.

'We must have a discussion on the Romantic era very soon,' he whispered, as he broke away to smile down into her eyes. 'It's good to know we agree on art and music, but let's concentrate on ourselves. Time is so precious, and I want to make you happy tonight, Lucinda. . .'

She sighed as his hands began to caress her shoulders, moving seductively down to fondle her breasts.

'This woollen dress is as good as a chastity belt,' he said, with a grin. 'Is there any chance you've brought the key along with you?'

Lucinda laughed. 'I hadn't envisaged a seduction scene when I went on duty this morning!'

Suddenly he stood up and pulled her to her feet. Minus her shoes she felt very tiny and helpless as he scooped her up into his arms. 'I've got a better idea. We'd be much more comfortable in the bedroom.'

She was aware of his eyes upon her as he spoke. . .of the unspoken question between them. She smiled her acquiescence and closed her eyes in joyful oblivion as she felt herself being carried, as if on a wave of passion, into the bedroom. Oh, yes, she was sure this was what she wanted. She had never wanted anything more in her whole life. She had never met anyone she loved like this wonderful man.

Her senses registered soft lights beside the wide bed on which Jonathan gently laid her. Her dress had somehow magically disappeared. When she felt the touch of his bare skin against hers she sighed with excitement and mounting desire. His hands gently caressing her breasts were sending sensations of pure pleasure through her entire body, and she arched her back as she strained to become closer with him. She knew she wanted nothing less than total union. She wanted him to possess her, to fulfil her in a way she had never been fulfilled before. She could feel their increasing passion as they clung to each other, their lips joined as their bodies moved in rhythmic harmony towards the ultimate climax that was pure magic.

Afterwards they lay back amid the tangled cotton sheets, their arms around each other. Lucinda's head was on Jonathan's chest and she lay absolutely still, savouring the heavenly moment. She hadn't believed love could be so wonderful. Nothing in her life had ever prepared her for the rapture she had just experienced, and the glow of happiness which enveloped her. Her eyelids felt heavy; her languorous body seemed to yearn for even more relaxation as she gave in to the deep desire for sleep.

* * *

She was awakened by the shrilling of the telephone. At first she was unable to remember where she was. But the sensual situation came back to her as she heard Jonathan's urgent voice. She smiled as she watched him in the half light of the bedside lamp. He looked strangely unfamiliar, but totally desirable, wrapped in a huge white cotton sheet. Suddenly her relaxed mood started to evaporate as her mind began to decipher the conversation.

'I'm on my way. . .yes, I'll contact Dr Barrymore,' she heard him say, in a brusque voice.

She tried to sit up, but half of the sheet was round Jonathan's chest. It would have seemed ludicrous if she hadn't seen the serious look on his face.

He put down the phone and leaned across to brush his lips against hers. 'We've got to go, my darling,' he whispered. 'No regrets, I hope?'

She put her hands around the back of his neck and pulled him towards her again. 'Only that we have to go so soon. What's the problem?'

He turned away and moved rapidly across the room. 'Get dressed quickly. There's been a minibus crash in the Mile End Road—a party of children and teachers. We've been asked to take them as we're the nearest to the scene of the crash and we've got enough beds. The first ambulance has arrived already.'

From long years of training Lucinda found it easy to switch herself into top gear when necessary. It was a matter of minutes before they were racing back to hospital along the Embankment. Lucinda looked across at Jonathan and thought that it was as if the romantic interlude had never happened.

Indeed, as they approached the main doors of the hospital and saw the flashing lights and heard the loud sirens of the ambulances she began to wonder if the whole experience had been a dream. . .a wonderful, improbable dream.

Her mind was fully alert as they raced into Accident and Emergency. The duty officer looked up with relief from the child he was examining.

'Fractured pelvis, sir,' he told Jonathan briefly, holding up the X-rays to confirm the diagnosis.

'How many empty orthopaedic beds do we have on Children's Surgical?' Jonathan asked Lucinda.

'Six, but we can easily convert more if necessary.'

'This little boy will need to be immobilised in a pelvic cradle initially. Will you set that up while I check out the rest of the casualties?'

'Of course.' Lucinda waved a hand at one of the porters, asking him to bring over a trolley.

Minutes later, her young patient was in the capable hands of the sister on Children's Surgical. It seemed strange to be returning to the scene of so much Christmas happiness with this small, frightened boy. Lucinda had managed to soothe him, but he was still asking for his mother. As soon as she had fixed up the pelvic sling she sat down beside the boy's bed and took hold of his hand.

'How old are you, Raymond?' she asked gently.

'Eleven, miss. When will my mum get here?'

'We've sent messages to all your parents. They shouldn't be long now. That medicine I gave you will make you feel sleepy, and you'll be able to have some rest before your mum gets here.'

She looked down at the little boy and stretched out a hand to smooth back the tousled red hair. His face was smeared from wiping away the tears.

'My mum was going to come with us on our trip,' the boy whimpered. 'But she had to look after my gran. We're all from East Cross Junior School. We went over the other side of London to some old people's home to sing carols. Then they gave us some supper and we were all happy and singing on the way home. . .and then this big car shot across in front of us. . . I think he must have jumped the lights, because I remember noticing that they were green for us, and then. . .when's my mum coming, miss?'

Lucinda squeezed the little boy's hand. 'Very soon, Raymond. Try and go to sleep—it'll make the time go quicker.' She tucked the sheet up around his chest before standing up. 'I'll come back and see you as soon as I can.'

She was relieved to see Raymond's eyes beginning to close as she moved off across the ward to speak to Sister. The lights had been dimmed, but some of the little patients were staring wide-eyed into the semi-darkness.

'Go to sleep,' Lucinda whispered to one of the little girls who had followed her around during the Christmas festivities, only hours before.

'I want my mummy!' the little girl wailed, holding out her arms towards Lucinda.

Lucinda sat down and calmed the lonely child,

talking to her in a soothing voice until she agreed to close her eyes and try to sleep again.

She went back to Sister's desk. 'What sort of provision do we have for parents to stay with their children?' she asked quietly.

In the light of the desk lamp she saw the Sister give a puzzled frown. 'You must be joking! We've barely enough beds for the patients without giving bed and breakfast to the relatives!'

In spite of her new-found feeling of mellowness towards Jonathan, Lucinda could feel the familiar surge of professional annoyance. It was archaic not to provide room for the relatives when their very presence could speed up the recovery period of young patients. She would have to do something about it. . .but not now!

Not now, when there was so much to be done. . .and when, if she was honest with herself, she was loath to shatter the wonderful rapport that existed between her and Jonathan.

As she hurried back down the corridor a tingling feeling of sensual pleasure suddenly swept over her. Even in the midst of all this distress she couldn't calm the excitement that Jonathan had stirred inside her. But that was Jonathan, the man, the lover, the most wonderful. . .

She checked her romantic thoughts as she reached Accident and Emergency and looked around her. The stern consultant bending over one of the small patients bore no resemblance to the man of her dreams.

Jonathan looked up and frowned. 'You took your

time. I want you to assist me. This little girl is called Jenny.' He moved away from the patient and spoke with a quiet urgency. 'She's got a mid-shaft fracture of femur. Sister's setting up a theatre for us because we'll have to insert a Steinmann's pin behind the tibial tubercule so that we can immobilise the limb with a Thomas's splint and put her on skeletal balanced traction.'

Lucinda nodded. 'How many casualties do we have?'

Jonathan swept an arm in the direction of the crowded department. 'There were twelve children in the minibus and two teachers. Those who are not badly injured are in a state of shock, so they'll need to be hospitalised for the night.'

'And the relatives? What's happening about them?'

He stared at her with a puzzled look. 'That's the least of our worries. The police are informing them and bringing in those who can make it. When they've seen their children they'll go home, of course, and. . .'

'Why of course?' she countered. 'Why can't they stay here to be near their children?'

He ran a hand through his tousled dark hair in a gesture of profound impatience. 'Because we simply haven't got provision for them. They're welcome to stay in the waiting-room if. . .'

'Would you stay in the waiting-room?' she flung at him, her blue eyes blazing angrily. 'Would you camp down on a couple of hard chairs until. . .'

'This is neither the time nor the place for a full-scale argument on hospital policy, Lucinda,' he hissed, under his breath. 'For heaven's sake, control yourself and get along to theatre before I lose my temper with you! Sometimes I think you deliberately pick a quarrel for the sake of it!'

She opened her mouth to make a retort, but thought better of it. 'I'll be in theatre when you require me, sir,' she muttered, turning away before she had time to say something she might regret. So much for not shattering the romantic rapport!

There was an air of expectancy when she walked into the theatre, gowned and masked. She had struggled once more out of the red dress, deciding that she was going to consign it to the local charity shop when she got back to her room! It had been the longest Christmas Day she ever remembered.

She looked up over the top of her mask at the theatre clock and realised that they had reached the small hours of Boxing Day morning. Time had ceased to mean anything to her.

Jonathan barely glanced at her when he swept in through the swing doors to take his place across the other side of the small patient.

'Our little patient, Jenny Gardner, age ten, has sustained a mid-shaft fracture of femur,' he announced in a weary voice that was utterly devoid of his usual flamboyancy.

Lucinda looked around the theatre and saw that, even at this unearthly hour, there were a few eager-beaver medical students, their eyes glued on the great man's hands as he made the first incision. She remembered how she had been just the same in her student days, joining in and helping in all the major emergencies so as to get valuable experience. None of it had been wasted. She was glad she had worked hard before she qualified. . .if only so that she could stand her own ground with egomaniacs like Jonathan Rathbone!

'Are you with us, Dr Barrymore?' the great man enquired, in an acid tone. 'Would it be possible for you to hold this retractor very steady so that I can insert the Steinmann's pin?'

She made a massive effort to concentrate, even though her eyelids felt as if they were made of sandbags.

Keep going, Lucinda, she told herself as she threaded a cannula to make the final sutures. There had been some peripheral damage to the tissues of the upper leg that required surgical intervention, and Jonathan was applying himself totally to the reduction of the fracture while she worked on the subsidiary injuries.

She raised herself and looked across the table as she made the final suture, realising that Jonathan had been watching her. The eyes that regarded her over the top of his mask held none of the tenderness she had seen earlier. He turned his head away and spoke briefly to the theatre sister.

'She's all yours. She can go back to the ward and I'll be along as soon as I can to check on the traction.'

Lucinda pulled at her mask, feeling suddenly impossibly weary and longing for some air. As she started to move away from the table she heard Jonathan's voice.

'Dr Barrymore, I'd like a word.'

She turned back, her heart thumping, but not with any romantic notions. She recognised when Jonathan was furious with her by the icy tone of his voice.

She fell into step with him as they went along the corridor. 'I think you'd better go off duty,' he told her brusquely. 'I've got enough staff to cope with the rest of the new patients, and I can't stand any of your wild ideas being flung out in the middle of a full-scale emergency.'

Lucinda stopped in her tracks, checking that the corridor was deserted before calling after the departing figure, 'I won't give up, Jonathan! I believe I'm right and you're wrong. . .just as you were wrong when you wouldn't allow my friend Julia to have her baby naturally. She told me how you forced her to take sedatives before the baby was born, how you. . .'

'That's enough! How dare you question my medical integrity!' He was striding back towards her, his dark eyes blazing with fury. 'I've had just about enough of your interference! What's this mythical case you're talking about? Who's Julia?'

Lucinda stood her ground, although she was terrified of the dangerous look in Jonathan's eyes. She already regretted blurting out her accusations at this inopportune time when they were both exhausted. It had been her intention to sound him out about the case when she found a suitable situation, but her anger and weariness had got the better of her. She'd jumped the gun and she'd have to see it through.

'Julia Lazelle is an old school friend of mine. She came in to hospital in September knowing exactly how she wanted her baby to be delivered. She specifically asked. . .'

'I remember her,' he cut in icily. 'Tall girl with auburn hair.' He paused, his eyes narrowing ominously as he stared down at her. 'I've no comment to make.'

'But you knew she wanted a natural birth! She'd attended classes and spent all her ante-natal time preparing for the birth. She's a very intelligent woman, and she told me how you intervened and countermanded all her requests.'

There was a noise at the far end of the corridor as a trolley bore down upon them. One of the new patients was being transferred to a ward.

'I'd like you to go off duty, Doctor,' Jonathan said coldly. 'And that's an order.'

CHAPTER ELEVEN

IN THE weeks that followed their blazing row Jonathan was deliberately polite to Lucinda, but she could tell that all the warmth and feeling he had shown towards her had vanished. She deeply regretted accosting him as she had done when neither of them was in a fit state to conduct a balanced argument. If she'd planned to pick the worst time possible she'd certainly succeeded!

But at least she had got it off her chest, she told herself as she went about her medical duties one cold February morning. She had felt incensed about the case ever since her friend Julia had broken down and cried when she had described her childbirth experience last September. Someone had to tell Jonathan that he couldn't ride roughshod over the wishes of the mothers—especially a super-intelligent woman like Julia. The only thing was, Lucinda wished it hadn't fallen to her lot to be the one to tell him!

She shivered as she pushed open the door of Children's Surgical. But she knew it wasn't the cold of the corridor that had given her the shivers. Oh, no! It was the awful memory of Jonathan's anger when he had ordered her to go off duty. She thought she would never forget the look in his eyes, and coming so soon after their magical interlude it had been even harder to bear. Because, if she was honest with herself, she knew that her personnel feelings hadn't changed. She couldn't stop loving the wretched man even though their professional ideas were poles apart. And there was no likelihood of their ever getting together again. Jonathan had made that absolutely clear whenever they had been forced to work together. He had been called away to a medical conference and she hadn't seen him now for a couple of weeks. In many ways she had found it easier to get on with her work without the emotional confusion she felt every time he came near her.

She looked around the ward while she waited for Sister to bring up the inspection trolley. It was good to see that all the patients from the minibus crash had been well enough to be discharged. Only young Jenny Gardner was still on traction, waiting for her mid-shaft fracture of femur to heal.

Lucinda smiled at the young patient as she adjusted the weights on the pulley. Holding up the latest X-rays against the light, she could see a definite improvement in the healing process.

'Won't be long now, Jenny. You'll soon be able to go home,' she told the girl.

'I wish my mum could come and stay with me for a bit,' Jenny replied wistfully. 'She said she misses me as much as I miss her. My dad's in the Army and he's overseas at the moment, so Mum's all on her own like me.'

'You're not on your own,' Lucinda replied, with a joviality she didn't feel. Poor little mite! she was thinking. It's rotten being separated like this.

She hadn't dared to broach the subject of relatives being allowed to stay again. Not since the awful night of her row with Jonathan. Some of the fight had gone out of her. She would probably only stay to the end of her short contract, so she found herself wondering if it was worth the aggro.

She patted the young patient's hand and turned away, telling herself that of course it was worth it. No one would ever achieve anything if they gave up when the going got tough. Maybe she should have a word with Dr Mary. Now there was a battling old reformer for you! In her younger days, she must have worked hard to achieve so much. Yes, that was what she'd do; go over to see the old lady before her impossible son got back from London.

Sister arrived with the inspection trolley and Lucinda pushed the thoughts to the back of her mind. For the next hour she was fully occupied caring for all her little patients, but as soon as she left the ward she felt the familiar surge of excitement that always helped to carry her through a difficult assignment.

She left her white coat in the staff common-room, pulled on a warm jacket and went out of the hospital through the back entrance of the X-ray department. A brisk walk across the path to the Rathbone residence was just what she needed.

There had been a mild spell of weather in the middle of February, and she was amused to see that the primroses had been fooled into opening out ahead of time. She took in some deep breaths of fresh air as she walked along the path. It was good to be alive on a day like this. Who needed the emotional problems of romance? Certainly she didn't!

Some of her happiness evaporated as she stood on the step waiting for the door to be opened. She hadn't seen Dr Mary since Christmas Day. . .not since she had learned the truth about her mother. . .and she wasn't sure how she would be received.

'You'd better come in, then,' said the housekeeper in response to her request to see Dr Mary. 'But don't stay long, because she's had the flu and she gets tired easily.'

She was shown into the drawing-room. As she looked towards the fireplace, she felt as if she was experiencing a flashback. Sitting on either side of the fireplace were mother and son, intent on reading their books.

Jonathan looked up in surprise and stood up, moving towards her with a puzzled look in his dark eyes.

'Lucinda! What on earth are you doing here?'

She hesitated, feeling again the same sense of being unwelcome that she had experienced on her first visit. 'I could ask you the same question,' she replied. 'I thought you were in London.'

'The conference finished early, so I decided to take a couple of days' holiday and make sure that Mother had recovered from her illness. Is there a problem at the hospital?'

'No. . .not exactly.'

His eyes clouded over. 'How do you mean, not exactly? Either there is or there isn't.'

'Come and sit by the fire, Lucinda,' Dr Mary called. 'Jonathan, take Lucinda's coat and ask Hilda to bring us some coffee.'

As she felt the touch of his fingers on her shoulders Lucinda almost shivered with the remembered sensation of that night in Jonathan's apartment. When he had taken off her coat that night. . .how many weeks ago was it? It seemed like a lifetime.

Mrs Banks brought in the coffee and Lucinda bided her time as they all made polite small talk.

Jonathan was the first to make his impatience obvious. 'Now come on, Lucinda, there must be a problem, otherwise you wouldn't have trekked across here.'

As she put down her cup she could almost hear them telling her that she was persona non grata in the Rathbone house and hospital. She'd poked her nose in where she wasn't wanted, and her intervention today was the last straw.

She took a deep breath as she fixed her eyes on Jonathan. 'It's the problem I spoke to you about at Christmas. The more I work with the children here, the more I realise how much we need facilities for relatives to stay and be near their loved ones. We give the patients all the tender loving care we can, but it's not enough!'

She broke off, intensely aware that her voice had risen to a higher pitch than she intended. The room seemed ominously quiet, the silence disturbed only by the crackling of the fire and the ticking of the antique grandfather clock.

'As I explained before,' Jonathan began, in a quiet, restrained voice, 'we have barely enough beds for the patients. Short of asking the relatives to bring their own tents and camp out on the forecourt. . .'

'Don't be silly, Jonathan!' Dr Mary's interruption took them both by surprise. 'Lucinda has got a valid point. The days of set visiting times are over.'

Lucinda watched wide-eyed as Jonathan rounded on his mother.

But what do you suggest we do, Mother?'

The old lady shook her head. 'I've no idea. Perhaps Lucinda has been giving more thought to the problem than we have. Have you come up with a solution, my dear?'

Moved by the warmth of the old lady's voice, Lucinda decided to take the bull by the horns. An idea had been forming over the past few weeks, but she had hardly dared to admit it even to herself, and she was sure that the Rathbones would think she was mad!

Oh, well, here goes! she thought, as she stood up and moved over to the window, looking out across the vast expanse of garden.

'I've been thinking for some time that you might consider using some of your own property. This house and garden are surely much too big for you. If you were to give some of it over to the hospital we could provide sleeping accommodation for relatives. The children could have their mothers with them, and this would speed up their recovery.'

She looked across the room, her eyes wide with bravado. There! She'd got it off her chest and they could do their worst to her!

Jonathan stood up and strode across the room to stand looking down at her, with a puzzled frown on his face. 'Are you serious about this hare-brained scheme?'

'I would like to be,' she replied firmly. 'Of course, we can do nothing without your mother's permission.' She looked across at Dr Mary.

The old lady's expression gave nothing away. Lucinda deduced that she was probably deciding to ask her to leave as soon as possible!

After a few seconds Dr Mary gave a slow smile. 'I have to admit that I've been thinking a little along the same lines myself. You see, my father left a sizeable amount of money to be used to found the hospital, but he specified that I was to make ample provision for myself. I was to maintain this old house in the way that he had done. I've never been sure how to get round that clause in his will, but if I were merely to take in relatives as my guests, I don't think I'd be going against his wishes. But the whole scheme would have to be organised properly, and I'm too old and tired to sort it out myself.'

'I could do it!' Lucinda said eagerly.

The old lady smiled. 'I'm sure you could, my dear. I expect you could move mountains if you had to! You know, you remind me very much of how I was at your age. . .full of hope and vision. Don't let anyone take that away from you.'

'Oh, I won't!' Lucinda assured her with feeling.

'Well, I give you permission to work out a scheme and present Jonathan with the details. If he thinks it's acceptable you can go ahead. I'll pick up all the bills within reason. Don't go spoiling the relatives, mind. I mean, if they want to stay at the Ritz, it's just across town.'

Lucinda's eyes met Jonathan's. She fully expected him to remonstrate, but he was strangely quiet. At length he spoke.

'We'll have to do something about the path from the hospital—it gets very muddy during the winter. I think I'll get it raised up from the ground and have it widened. What do you think, Lucinda?'

She didn't trust herself to speak. She wanted to tell him that this was the first time he had come round to her way of thinking and he'd created a welcome precedent. Was he now going to acquiesce to all her professional demands during the short time that she would remain here?

At the thought of how little time she had left she felt a pang of dismay. If only. . .if only they could work out some of their other differences there might still be a future together for them. Because she knew, without a doubt, that she had never loved anyone so much as she loved this man. . .but not this doctor!

She opened her mouth to reply to his question and found that her tongue had gone dry. 'I think an improvement to the path would be an excellent idea.'

'Come over here, my dear,' said Dr Mary, in a quiet voice. 'I know you think I'm a spoilt old lady with everything that money can buy, but it wasn't always like this. Oh, dear, no! Even Jonathan doesn't know how hard my life used to be.'

Lucinda went back across the room and seated herself on the sofa, her eyes on the old lady. She was vaguely aware that Jonathan had joined her on the other end of the sofa, but she deliberately avoided looking in his direction.

'I'm not sure that Lucinda would be interested in your early life, Mother, and I expect she's got to get back to hospital,' Jonathan said in a gentle tone.

'On the contrary, I'm extremely interested, Dr Mary,' Lucinda put in hastily, ignoring Jonathan. 'And I've done everything I need to do this morning. Please go on.'

The old lady smiled and a faraway look came in her eyes. I haven't always lived in this grand house. My father, Dr Jeremiah Rathbone, had a small country practice in Somerset. When I was five, my mother, who loved riding, fell from a horse, fractured her skull and sustained a serious injury to the brain.'

Lucinda drew in her breath in sympathy as she saw the pain that registered on the old lady's face. It was obvious that even after all these years the tragedy still lived on in her mind. She glanced at Jonathan and he turned towards her. In his eyes she thought she detected some of the warmth and tenderness he had shown towards her all those weeks ago. Her pulses quickened and she turned away to concentrate all her attention on Dr Mary's sad story.

But she was intensely aware of the dark eyes scutinising her, and she could almost feel the touch of those long, tantalising fingers only inches away from her.

'In those days there was little that could be done for an injury as severe as my mother's. The brain specialist advised my father to have my mother put in a mental insitution, but he refused. He loved her very much and he couldn't bear to think of her spending the rest of her life locked up. So he hired a couple of nurses to look after her. The added expense of nurses' fees and the general distraction of the situation meant that we became more and more impoverished.'

The old lady gave a sad smile and leaned forward. 'I hope I'm not boring you, Lucinda. Perhaps this isn't the time to reminisce, but I wanted you to see why it was that my father put a clause in his will to ensure that I take care of myself in my later years.'

'Please go on,' Lucinda urged, intrigued.

'Yes, do go on, Mother. I don't think I've ever heard the full story.'

Lucinda was aware that Jonathan had moved closer towards her on the sofa, and she could feel her heart beginning to thump loudly. The combination of Dr Mary's confiding in her and Jonathan's physical proximity was unnerving.

The old lady leaned back in her chair, closing her eyes as if to get a better picture of those far-off events. 'It was the sort of medical practice where many of the rural patients were slow to pay their bills. They paid when they could, or they brought round some eggs or a couple of chickens. But many of them simply forgot, and my father, who had no interest in the financial side of the practice, could barely make ends meet.'

Dr Mary opened her eyes and leaned forward again. 'So when I was fourteen, I insisted on leaving school so that I could take things into my own hands. I'd been running the house after a fashion since I was about eight, and I decided that if we got rid of the nurses I could do a much better job and we'd be that much better off. My father was too weary to argue with me, and when he found that things were getting better under my management he started to enjoy life again. My mother, who had been positively violent with the nurses, was much calmer with me. She didn't know who I was, but. . .'

'She didn't know you were her daughter?' Jonathan queried. 'You've never told me that before.'

His mother smiled a strange secret smile. 'There are many things I haven't told you. No, your grandmother didn't know who I was from the day of her accident. And when I was small she couldn't stand me. She used to shriek whenever I went near her. But after I left school and was in sole charge of her we became very close. I'm glad I had those few years with her. . .heartbreaking as it was to see her like that.'

'But how did you manage to get to medical school?' Lucinda asked.

'I'm coming to that,' the old lady replied. 'It looked as if I would have to look after my mother until she died, and I was quite prepared to do that, because I'd never seen such a transformation in my father. From being a downtrodden, overworked man he became once more the young, interesting father I'd loved as a child before Mother had her accident. He was an extremely good doctor, and he was often called upon to attend the local squire. Now here was a man who always paid his bills. Sometimes he used to call in to the surgery and come along to see me. "Mary," he used to say, "you ought not to be cooped up here wearing yourself to a shadow like this. What would you really like to do if you could get away from all this domestic drudgery?"'

Dr Mary leaned forward with a smile on her lips, her eyes dancing mischievously. 'And I used to tell him my dream was to become a doctor like my father and my grandfather, but I knew that was out of the question because I had to look after Mother.' The old lady drew in her breath. 'When I was eighteen, the squire died, and when the will was read it transpired he'd left everything to my father with the express wish that I was to train to be a doctor.'

'How wonderful!' Lucinda breathed. 'So who looked after your mother?'

The old lady smiled happily. 'My father decided we could get the best attention for her in London, and he could be near me while I studied at medical school. We now had plenty of money, so we moved to this house. He no longer needed to work, and he was very happy to stay at home and care for my mother with the help of some excellent, specially trained nurses.'

She paused and her eyes narrowed shrewdly as she fixed them on Lucinda. 'But he took a vicarious pleasure in following my medical career, and he was always intensely interested in what I was doing. I remember badgering him about the need for a hospital for women and children. . .rather in the way you started on at me this morning. He used to listen, with a tolerant look on his face, but I thought it would all come to nothing. Anyway, when he died—just a month after my mother—he left everything to me, saying that I could use the money to found a hospital if I wished, but that I was to leave enough to keep this place going and have an easier life than I'd had in my early years. . . There now! That's how it was, so you understand my initial reluctance to jump at your idea, Lucinda.'

Lucinda flashed her a grateful smile. 'You're very kind, Dr Mary. I do appreciate it. I envisage some kind of self-contained wing would be the best plan, don't you?'

'Who for? The relatives or Mother?' Jonathan asked quickly.

'Oh, for the relatives, of course,' Lucinda replied.

Dr Mary put up her hand and shook her head. 'Let the relatives have the run of the main house. I'll have a self-contained flat. I don't need much space.'

Jonathan smiled. 'We'll work something out and show you the plans, Mother.' He turned to look at Lucinda.

She moved nervously on the sofa as his eyes focused directly on her. It was the first time she had actually looked him in the face since that fateful night when he had literally banished her from the hospital. And she found herself falling again. . .falling oh, so hopelessly in love with this infuriating man.

'When would it be convenient for us to meet to discuss the alterations? I've got another day off tomorrow. When are you free?' he asked in a deliberately professional voice.

'I'll have to check the duty roster when I get back to the common-room,' she replied, standing up.

He got to his feet and looked down at her with a disarming smile. 'I'll call you this evening.'

CHAPTER TWELVE

LUCINDA raced back along the path to the hospital. Her feet felt as if they were attached to magic wings! She seemed as light as a fairy and as excited as a child on Christmas morning. She tried to tell herself that the sole reason for her elation was that she had been given the green light for her relatives project, but she knew that at least half her happiness stemmed from the mellowing attitude of Dr Jonathan Rathbone.

She smiled to herself as she remembered the look in his eyes when he had said goodbye at the door. It would be hard to describe those eyes and do them justice, she thought. They had such depth, such warmth when he was in a good mood. . .and such ice and frost when he was displeased!

But today he had thawed out. Their cold war of the last few weeks was at an end. Well, it was on her part anyway. . .until the next time he decided to cross her. She remembered how he had told her not to question his medical integrity. She knew how he felt about that one, because she too had her own ideals. And the awful problem was that they were so different from Jonathan's.

Compromise, that was what was needed, she decided, but put the idea to the back of her mind. She had always considered compromise was for cowards, or wishy-washy people who couldn't make up their own minds.

Still smiling, she went in through the back entrance and hurried round the corner of the X-ray unit, past the Path Lab, along the corridor that led to Outpatients, and then she swung into the staff common-room.

'You look happy,' Sister Bradwell remarked, as she passed her in the doorway.

'It's that sort of day,' Lucinda said vaguely. 'Spring is in the air and the primroses are peeping out already.'

Cynthia Bradwell gave her a knowing smile. 'Are you sure that's all that's in the air?'

Lucinda's smile broadened, but she made no reply as she went across the room to retrieve her white coat. She was aware that Sister Bradwell was still watching her.

'Any chance of a visit this afternoon, Dr Barrymore? I've got a new obstetrics patient who's proving a bit difficult. You know the kind I mean. She's got a list of don'ts that she wants us to adhere to when we're delivering her baby. No painkillers, no episiotomy, no forceps; just dim lights and bean-bags. I'd ask Dr Rathbone to see her, but he's still away, apparently.'

'I'll come and see her,' Lucinda said quickly. 'I might be more attuned to her demands than Dr Rathbone will be. She sounds like the type who'll drive him demented!'

Sister Bradwell laughed. 'It takes more than a

difficult patient to upset the boss. It's difficult staff who infuriate him.'

Lucinda turned round. 'Meaning what, Sister?'

Cynthia Bradwell looked sheepish. 'Oh, I think you know what I mean. It's all round the hospital how you two had a tiff at Christmas. One of the porters came across you in the corridor and he said you were going at it hammer and tongs. At first he thought it was just a lovers' tiff, but then. . .' The sister stopped in embarrassment. 'I shouldn't have said that. Please. . .'

'Said what?' Lucinda opened her eyes deliberately wide. 'I didn't hear what you said. I'll come along to the ward immediately after lunch, Sister.'

So it was all round the hospital, was it? she thought as she heard Sister Bradwell retreating down the corridor. She wondered what sense the rest of the staff were making of their on-off romance. Probably more than she was herself!

She found herself becoming increasingly aware of the glances in her direction when she went into the staff dining-room. It occurred to her that there must have been more idle speculation than she'd realised. But that was all it was. . .idle speculation, because she was light years away from resolving her differences with Jonathan. But she could dream, couldn't she? She could dream about a man who resembled Jonathan in every way except that he wasn't a doctor. What would she have him be? She knew very little about men who were outside the medical profession.

She found she was smiling as she sat down at one

of the less crowded tables and she had to deliberately compose her features. The conversation, as usual, was mostly shop. Today, she thought how strange it was that the medical profession were able to discuss detailed anatomical descriptions while eating lunch.

Cynthia Bradwell was waiting for her when she got to the ward. It seemed to Lucinda that the sister was being deliberately professional to counteract her tactless slip before lunch.

'This is the patient I was telling you about, Dr Barrymore,' Sister told her, as they made towards one of the ante-natal cubicles.

Lucinda was briefly introduced to the patient before Sister left them alone. She glanced at the notes before sitting down on the bedside chair. 'So you came in early this morning, but it was a false alarm, Mrs Dawson, am I right?'

The patient smiled. 'That's correct, Doctor. I was sure I was having contractions. . . I mean, I've studied the subject of childbirth in great detail, so you'd think I would have known.'

Lucinda smiled back. 'Contractions are not all that easy to recognise, especially if it's your first baby. On the one hand we have patients rushing in with a false alarm and others who confuse the situation with mere backache and finish up delivering themselves on the bathroom floor! It's often better to err on the cautious side as you did.'

'I expect I'd be able to deliver myself if I had to,' the patient announced confidently. 'You see, I've learned such a lot since I decided to become pregnant. Even before I conceived, my husband and I had gone into training. He, of course, will be with me throughout the delivery.'

Lucinda made no comment as she stood up. 'I'd like to examine you, Mrs Dawson. Just relax now.'

At the end of the examination, Lucinda assured her patient that there was no evidence of contractions, but that the foetus was engaged and in a healthy condition. 'I expect your baby will start to arrive within the next few days when it's good and ready.' She glanced down at the notes. 'You don't live too far away, so you could go home.'

'Oh, no, Doctor. Now that I'm here I want to absorb the atmosphere of the place where baby will be born and make final preparations. I've written out my baby birth plan for you to read. I want to make sure that all the staff adhere to my requests when the time comes.'

Lucinda took the folder of papers that was handed to her. She skipped through the first few pages, which had been copied from a book on natural childbirth, and she was familiar with the contents. It was when she came to the last couple of pages that she began to feel somewhat disturbed. Her patient had made a list of don'ts about the birth. Some of them seemed reasonable, but others could be tricky if there was a real emergency.

'I see you've forbidden us to use forceps or to perform an episiotomy,' she remarked.

The patient nodded.

'And you don't want the cord cut until after it's stopped pulsating, and after the birth no one must feed the baby except you.'

'You've got it, Doctor. I shall breast-feed my baby so that I can establish a good feeding pattern from the outset.'

'Yes, I see,' Lucinda said evenly. Why was it that she was having such feelings of apprehension about this case? She agreed in principle with everything that the patient had requested, but no one could predict how the delivery would go until it actually started.

She peeled off her surgical gloves and tossed them on to the lower shelf of the trolley, before striding over to scrub her hands vigorously in the corner sink unit. She turned off the mixer tap with her white-coated sleeve, still unsure of how she should handle the situation.

'I'll certainly give your instructions to the rest of the staff,' she told her patient.

'Including Dr Rathbone, my consultant?'

'Especially your consultant,' Lucinda replied, hoping that he wouldn't be around when the baby decided to appear.

'What's Dr Rathbone really like?' the patient asked. 'When I discussed my ideas with him he was very noncommittal. . .told me we'd deal with the situation when the time came. Oh, and he said he didn't know whether you had any bean-bags for me to relax on during the delivery, and I got the impression he wasn't going to try and find one.'

'I think you might have to ask your husband to bring one in, Mrs Dawson,' Lucinda hastily. 'Dr Rathbone is an exceptionally efficient obstetrician, but he does insist on his own methods. However, I'll be on hand to help you when you need me.'

Kitty Dawson smiled. 'Thanks, Doctor. Will there be a room where my husband can sleep tonight?'

Lucinda smiled. 'I'm afraid not, but, as I said, you could go home if you want to.'

'Oh, no,' the patient replied emphatically. 'I've got a lot of preparations to make and I need to practise my breathing. Besides which, I don't want to confuse my baby with too much to-ing and fro-ing.'

'Well, I'll see you later, then.' Lucinda drew back the curtains and hurried off down the ward, pausing only to have a quick word with Cynthia Bradwell.

'Let's hope Jonathan stays off duty until after this one is born,' she whispered.

Sister Bradwell smiled. 'Thanks for checking her in. Can I count on you to be on hand when the contractions start?'

Lucinda gave a wry grin. 'I'll do my best.'

Her feet felt decidedly weary as she climbed the outside stairs to the staff quarters. It had been a long day and she planned to have a refreshing shower. But at the back of her mind she was deeply conscious of the fact that Jonathan had said he would call her. She knew that the rapid increase in her pulse rate had nothing to do with the exertion of climbing the stairs!

As she reached the door she thought she could hear the phone ringing. Oh, goodness! Where was her key? She plunged it into the lock, praying that the shrilling would continue. She crossed the room in easy strides, reached out her hand and it stopped!

He'll ring again, she told herself. He's sure to ring again. She decided to postpone the shower until after he'd rung.

An hour went by, while she tried to relax, skimming through some medical papers that had been waiting for her attention for days. She glanced at the clock. He wouldn't be ringing now; it was much too late.

Despondently she peeled off her clothes and climbed into the narrow shower cubicle. See if she cared! He couldn't be very keen if he only rang once. . .what was that?

With shampoo dripping down her face she stepped out of the shower and dripped her way across the carpet to the phone.

'Yes? Oh, it's you, Jonathan,' she said, trying to sound cool and collected. If he could only see her now! Thank goodness it wasn't television. 'What's that? Can you speak up, it's a bad line.' She looked across at the shower cubicle where water was cascading noisily down. 'Tomorrow, you say. . .? Well, I'm not sure if I can make it.'

'You said you were going to check the duty roster.' Jonathan sounded impatient. 'I thought you might enjoy a whole day away from hospital. We could sort out most of our ideas if we had plenty of time to ourselves.'

Lucinda's heart was thumping madly as she wondered which ideas he was referring to. Did he really care that much about her scheme to provide a place for the relatives, or did he have other plans too?

'I'm on call all day,' she told him. 'I can't see how I can get round that.'

'I can,' came his confident reply, and she sensed that he was smiling. 'I'll get one of the young locums to cover for you. I know one of my ex-students who would be pleased to get the experience of working here. And we won't go far away, so we can hurry back if there's an emergency.'

'Well, if you're really sure,' she replied, trying to remain calm. 'Where exactly do you plan we should go for this professional discussion?'

She heard the welcome sound of his laughter and felt a now familiar sensual *frisson* running down her spine.

'Who said anything about a professional discussion?' he said. 'I've spent the day drawing up plans for the conversion of the house. And I've contacted a building firm to have them improve the path. So once you've cast your eyes over the plans and agreed. . .'

Warning bells were ringing in her ears; she wasn't going to let him have all his own way about the conversion. She intended to do more than cast her eyes over the plans! But, for the moment, she was loath to dispel the sense of rapport between them.

'. . .we can enjoy ourselves,' Jonathan continued. 'It seems to me we've been avoiding each other since that silly quarrel at Christmas. And we did have something rather special between us, Lucinda. I've missed you.'

She swallowed. Suddenly the world seemed such a wonderful place. He'd missed her. . .but not half as much as she'd missed him!

'Are you still there, Lucinda?'

'Yes, I'm still here.' She drew in her breath. She wasn't going to tell him that it hadn't been a silly quarrel. Only the timing had been inappropriate. She still had to settle a score with him over his high-handed treatment of her friend. But it could wait. . .it could certainly wait until after tomorrow!

'I must admit I'd welcome a day off if you can organise it,' she told him, her tone sounding more breathless than she'd hoped.

'Leave it with me. I'll pick you up about ten. Give yourself a long lie-in—you've earned it!'

The line went dead. Praise indeed! Lucinda thought. Maybe her contract would be extended, after all!

CHAPTER THIRTEEN

It was virtually impossible to sleep late in the staff quarters. Lucinda abandoned the idea of a lie-in the next morning. The sound of feet hurrying past her door and ambulances screeching to a halt in the forecourt below was not conducive to a relaxing start to the day. But as she opened the curtains and looked out on the busy scene she felt grateful to Jonathan for having made the suggestion that she take things easy today. And it was wonderful to know that he'd fixed up a locum to do her work.

A tiny nagging doubt entered her mind. Suppose he hadn't managed to find anyone? She decided she'd better make a quick reconnoitre of the hospital.

When she got into the hospital she found she needn't have worried. Everything was under control. In the obstetrics ward, Kitty Dawson was practising her breathing exercises and there was no sign of an imminent birth. The doctor who had taken Lucinda's place was a keen young man, and after briefing him on her patients she went along to the dining-room, confident that he could cope.

She helped herself to a croissant with delicious apricot jam and some coffee. She didn't feel in the least bit hungry, but she didn't want to start fainting away before they had lunch. At the thought of lunch, the familiar excitement returned. Where would they have lunch? Would it be the intimate little restaurant just round the corner from Jonathan's apartment?

At the thought of his apartment, she felt a sensual thrill running through her body. What a fabulous evening they'd had together! What a pity it had been spoiled by their argument!

As she stood up to return to her room, Lucinda made a mental note not to be argumentative today. She wanted to enjoy herself. . .and she could think of nothing more delightful than a whole day with Jonathan. . .outside hospital!

It was difficult to decide what to wear. As she rifled through her wardrobe, she was thinking it would have been a help if she knew where they were going. In the end she selected her new navy gabardine double-breasted jacket over her red gabardine skirt, worn with a navy jersey turtleneck top. High heels were a must! she decided. On duty it was impracticable to wear anything higher than an medium heel, but she would really enjoy her extra inches today! And she wouldn't have to strain her neck to look up at Jonathan.

She studied her reflection in the mirror when she was absolutely ready. It was a long time since she had gone to such trouble but the effort had been worth it. At the very least it boosted her morale, and that was no bad thing when she was going to be with Jonathan all day.

As she hurried down the staircase, she found herself wondering if this was what was meant by power dressing! She'd certainly dressed to impress today. Her heels clicked noisily as she made her way across towards Jonathan's distinctive car.

He had just arrived and was climbing out of the driver's seat. He smiled down at her. 'Who's the smart young lady?'

Lucinda laughed. 'I do occasionally cast off my white coat!'

He gave her a wicked grin and moved closer to take both her hands in his. 'I know. . . I remember,' he said huskily.

She felt herself blushing and turned her head. 'I didn't know what to wear. If I'd known where we were going. . .'

'I thought we'd go for a long walk over the marshes down by the river,' he said in a deadpan voice.

She glanced down at her delicate shoes.

'Only joking!' he told her, opening up the passenger door.

She climbed in, feeling relieved, and Jonathan started the ignition. They were soon driving away from the City towards the motorway. It seemed a very short time before the scenery changed from dense urban to wide expanse of rural fields and woodlands. And then they were turning off the motorway and driving along a narrow road through Epping Forest.

Jonathan drove the car into a clearing at the side of the road and switched off the engine. Lucinda looked out of the window. All around her the tall, majestic trees reached up to the unseasonally cloudless blue sky. The sun, shining through the bud-bedecked branches, was doing its best to convince them that spring had arrived.

She turned to look at Jonathan. He was leaning closer towards her, a gentle smile on his lips.

'It's so good to get out of London,' she breathed. 'What I notice most about the country is the silence. Listen!'

Jonathan spoke after a few seconds. 'There's the sound of the city in the background—the constant humming of traffic and trains. We're still within striking distance of the hospital. That's what I like about this place—so near and yet so far.' He started to open his door. 'Let's walk!'

'So you weren't joking! I'd love to walk, but I wish you'd warned me.'

'No problem. I've brought Mother's wellies. I knew you wouldn't be prepared.'

'They've not such a bad fit,' Lucinda remarked as they sloshed through the mud.

He took hold of her hand when they got down to the stream. 'You'll never manage to jump this bit with your short legs. I think I'd better lift you over.'

She opened her mouth to protest, but he had already scooped her up into his arms. She held her breath as they balanced precariously on a stone in the middle of the stream. And then they were clear over to the other side.

She gave a sigh of relief and looked up enquiringly to see why he hadn't put her down. There was a tender expression in his eyes and her heart began to beat faster. His arms were tightening around her as he pulled her closer towards him. She felt sure he was going to kiss her, but instead he swung her down to the ground again.

She walked along the stream-side path, intensely aware of Jonathan being so close behind her, and annoyed by the fact that she had wanted him to kiss her just now. The touch of his arms against her body had roused hidden memories of the passion they had shared. And she knew just how much she wanted to be with him again.

She stopped in her tracks as a grey squirrel scampered across the path in front of her and climbed a tall beech tree.

'Look at that!' she whispered.

Jonathan put his hands on her shoulders and held her close against his chest as they watched together. His jacket had fallen apart and she was aware of the beating of his heart through the thin cotton of his shirt. She was wondering if the heartbeats were as rapid as her own, when he pulled her round to face him. His kiss was all the more sweet because it was unexpected. She closed her eyes as his arms tightened about her, and time seemed to stand still as they clung to each other.

'Lucinda darling,' he whispered. 'If only we could always be like this together!'

She stirred in his arms, smiling up into the dark eyes that held such love. . .yes, real love, she was sure of it!

His fingers were still entwined with hers as they crossed a narrow wooden bridge and followed the path back to the car. The calm and beauty of the forest was adding to her feeling of romance. The rest of the day stretched ahead of them. There was no need to rush things. They would take everything at a leisurely pace and maybe, at the end of their day together, they would finish up at Jonathan's apartment.

They got back to the car and Jonathan helped Lucinda to remove the muddy boots. They laughed together at the effort that was involved.

'I think you've brought half the forest with you,' Jonathan said as he gave a final tug. 'After all this strenuous activity we need some lunch.'

He drove her to a country pub at the edge of the forest. A log fire crackled in the hearth, sending out a delicious smell that was reminiscent of autumn leaves and pine cones. The dark oak beams in the walls and low ceilings were studded with gleaming horse brasses. Lucinda leaned against the high-backed wooden seat as she watched Jonathan buying the drinks at the bar. He looked so handsome in his casual clothes! She found him infinitely more desirable than in his pin-striped consultant suit that seemed to bring out the worst in her!

He brought her a glass of wine and sat down on the wooden seat beside her. His arm touched hers as he raised his glass and she turned towards him, revelling in the feeling of rapport between them.

'To us!' he said softly.

'That's what you said last time,' she reminded him. 'And we soon quarrelled. Perhaps we should change the toast.'

He put his finger under her chin and drew her face towards his. 'We won't quarrel again, Lucinda. I think maybe I've been a little. . .unreasonable with you on occasions.'

She stared up into his eyes. 'I don't believe I'm hearing this!'

He laughed. 'Perhaps some of your ideas are worth implementing. Take this relatives scheme, for instance. I've warmed to the project as I worked on it.'

Lucinda smiled happily. 'Talking of which, don't you think we should have a look at the plans for the scheme? After all, this is why we came out today, isn't it?'

Jonathan took both of her hands in his. 'Ostensibly, yes, but actually, I needed an excuse to be alone with you. . .away from the hospital, of course!'

She laughed. 'Of course. It's best we should meet on neutral territory.'

They ordered the dish of the day, which happened to be shepherd's pie. The barmaid brought it to the table and smiled indulgently at the way they were holding hands and looking into each other's eyes. Lucinda tried to take away her hand, but Jonathan's fingers wouldn't let her escape. Still holding each other with one hand, they picked up their forks and began to eat.

'If we let go of each other, we'll break the romantic spell,' Jonathan whispered in her ear.

Lucinda laughed. 'I can't believe you're that ogre of a consultant who delights in putting me down!'

He squeezed her hand. 'That's all in the past. We need to have a serious talk. So if you've had enough of the rural life, may I suggest we drift back to my place for the rest of the day?'

She nodded as she snuggled against him. There was no one to see them in their little wooden booth, and on impulse she reached up and kissed his cheek. He responded by moving his mouth towards hers and claiming her lips.

As she sank back against the high-backed seat, her senses were reeling. It was as if she'd just tasted the starter of a banquet. She couldn't wait for the romantic feast to follow!

'I think I should warn you, I've got some unexpected news for you,' Jonathan told her gently.

She gave a lazy smile, her mind barely registering what he had said. 'What kind of news?'

'I don't want to talk about it until we get back to my place. It concerns your father.'

She sat bolt upright, her mind focusing sharply once more. 'My father? You mean. . .'

'Your natural father,' he explained. 'My mother has some information about him. I thought it best if I approached you first.'

Her head began to swim round. 'But your mother told me my father was unknown!'

Jonathan stood up. 'Look, I don't want to discuss it here. Just be patient until we get back to the apartment.'

'Have you any idea what it's like trying to be patient when you throw out a crumb of information about someone I've trained myself to stop thinking about?' Her voice had begun to rise and she hastily lowered it lest she attract attention. 'You know all about your own father. . .'

She broke off in embarrassment, remembering what he had said about his own father having died before he was born.

He gave a sad smile. 'Don't worry—I've trained myself not to think about my father too. My mother insisted it should be like that. She refused to answer my questions about him when I was a child. As I told you, he was a doctor in the RAF. Apparently they were only married a few weeks before he was killed in a plane crash. It was ironic, because he'd come through the Second World War as a pilot only to die a few years later. I never knew him, of course.'

Lucinda felt ashamed of her outburst and willed herself to be patient, even though she felt she couldn't wait to get back to Jonathan's place. Two reasons now for her wild anticipation!

She stood up. 'Let's go now, Jonathan.'

He put out a detaining hand. 'Wait here for a moment while I call the hospital to check on our young locum. I feel he's my responsibility, and I'd hate to find there was some problem he couldn't handle.'

She nodded impatiently. It would set both their minds at rest and they would be able to relax more easily. While she waited she deliberately tried not to speculate about what Jonathan might reveal concerning her natural father. In many ways it had been easier to accept that no one knew who he was. But if Dr Mary had been keeping his identity secret. . .

She stared in dismay at the deep frown on Jonathan's face. 'Is there a problem?'

He grimaced. 'I'm afraid so. There's a patient on Obstetrics who's insisting on seeing one or other of us. Sister Bradwell can't pacify her.'

Lucinda groaned. 'Not Kitty Dawson, is it?'

'Yes. I understand you examined her yesterday.'

'But has she gone into labour? There was no sign of it this morning.'

'Sister Bradwell said that Mrs Dawson claims to be having contractions, but she can't find any evidence of it. But she won't stop complaining that she's being neglected. We'd better go back for a short time and sort it out. We can go along to the apartment when we've pacified everybody.'

'Look, I can handle it by myself,' Lucinda said quickly. 'Take me back to the hospital. There's no need for you to come on to the ward—after all, you've got an official day's holiday.'

Jonathan looked at her with a wry grin. 'I know you, Lucinda. You're trying to keep me out of the way, aren't you?'

She smiled. 'Am I that transparent? It's just that this patient is insisting on all sorts of conditions, and I think I can handle her better than you can.'

The grin expanded. 'Oh, you do, do you? Let's see how she responds to both of us being there.'

Dark storm clouds hung over London as they approached. Lucinda crouched down in the seat, wondering how she was going to cope with the combined strength of wills of her patient and Dr

Jonathan Rathbone. Looking at him across the car, as he focused his attention on the road, she thought he looked mild-mannered and easygoing. But she was sure everything would change when they were back on the ward again.

And she was right! Jonathan's voice could be heard all the way down the ward as he remonstrated with Mrs Dawson.

'My dear lady, while I have every sympathy with the ideals you've just expressed, I find it difficult to believe that you're more expert at delivering babies than I am. It is, after all, your first baby, whereas my current total runs into several figures. So kindly allow me to be in charge of the case.'

The patient refused to budge. 'I'm sorry, Dr Rathbone, but I insist you follow my birth plan. Dr Barrymore has agreed to it, and she's shown it to all the staff.'

'Indeed!' Jonathan's eyes blazed angrily as he turned to look at Lucinda. 'Why wasn't I informed?'

'You were on holiday, sir,' she replied, thinking how ludicrous the situation was. 'If I might have a word with you in private I'll explain. . .'

'You certainly will explain. . .and right here in front of the patient! Because I don't want her going into labour under the false illusion that we're puppets who respond to having our strings pulled. Explain to the patient that she must toe the line and do as she's told if we're to have a safe delivery.'

Lucinda drew in her breath. 'I'm afraid I can't do that, sir,' she said firmly. 'We have to take each case on its merits. Some mothers have very strong convictions, and I don't think we should try to dissuade them.'

She stared up into the dark angry eyes, wishing there had been another way out of this dilemma. Suddenly Jonathan turned and walked away down the ward. Pausing by the desk, he spoke to Sister Bradwell in a loud clear voice.

'Dr Barrymore is now in charge of this case, Sister.'

CHAPTER FOURTEEN

By the time Lucinda had examined Mrs Dawson and convinced her that she wasn't in labour, she realised that Jonathan wasn't going to return to the ward. She went out to the forecourt and saw that his car had gone. She decided she wouldn't give him the satisfaction of ringing up to find out where he was. He'd made it perfectly clear just now that their professional relationship was more important than their private one. So much for the romantic evening she'd envisaged!

She climbed the stairs and hurried into her room, tossing the high-heeled shoes into a corner. Curling up on the sofa, she switched on her small portable television and stared at it mindlessly for the next hour, hoping against hope that Jonathan would call.

She must have fallen asleep on the sofa, because she awoke, feeling cold and uncomfortable, as the shrilling of the phone cut into her restless dreams.

She reached out and grabbed the handset eagerly. It wasn't Jonathan. Sister Bradwell's voice brought her quickly back to reality.

'It's Mrs Dawson again, Doctor. Can you come and have a word with her?'

'What's the matter now?' Lucinda asked wearily.

'I think she really is going into labour at last.

There's only mild activity showing at the moment, but she insists you examine her.'

Lucinda drew in her breath, trying hard not to blame the patient for her split with Jonathan. She must remain professional about this case. 'I'm on my way,' she said.

She found her patient in a state of excitement.

'I know I'm in labour this time, Doctor,' Mrs Dawson announced happily. 'I just want you to confirm it for me.'

Lucinda scrubbed her hands and pulled on a pair of surgical gloves. An extensive examination revealed only mild contractions, but she felt as relieved as the patient that the labour had actually begun.

'The contractions will get stronger,' she explained. 'If they become too strong for you I can give you some medication.'

Mrs Dawson shook her head adamantly. 'No painkillers.'

'I'll come back to see you when things get moving,' Lucinda told her.

She decided to stay on in hospital, rather than go back to her room. It was after midnight and the strange calm of the night had descended on the dimly-lit wards. She went to the dining-room and had some supper with one of the night sisters.

An hour later when she returned to Obstetrics, Mrs Dawson had fallen asleep. The contractions were almost non-existent. Lucinda decided to go back to her room and get some sleep.

She woke next morning and was surprised to see

how late it was. Reaching for the phone, she rang Obstetrics and enquired about her patient. Night Sister informed her that the contractions were sluggish, but the patient was complaining loudly even though she was still only in the first stage of labour.

'I didn't want to waken you,' Sister explained. 'I think she's making a fuss about nothing. There's a long way to go yet. And anyway, you told me she wouldn't take painkillers.'

'I'm on my way,' Lucinda said hastily.

Mrs Dawson's anxious eyes lit up when Lucinda arrived. 'I'm in agony, Doctor. I don't know how to say this, but I really would like to take something for the pain. I'd no idea it would be this bad.'

'Let me check out what's happening first,' Lucinda replied firmly, getting no satisfaction from witnessing her patient dispensing with her ideals.

A quick examination revealed that the contractions were indeed sluggish, as Sister had intimated, but the most worrying aspect of the case was that the foetus had changed its position and was now lying in breech presentation.

'I'll ask Sister to give you some pethidine,' Lucinda said gently.

She turned as she heard someone coming in through the curtains. Jonathan was standing behind her and had heard what she'd said.

'How's it going, Dr Barrymore?' he asked quietly.

'Very slowly,' Lucinda replied.

He went to the bedside and patted Mrs Dawson's hand. 'Just be patient, my dear. Nature will take its course, and we'll do what we can to help things along.'

Lucinda stepped outside the curtains at the same time as Jonathan. She looked up into his face, uncertain of what to say.

'Would you like me to assist you,?' he asked.

Relief flooded through her. 'Yes, please. I'm afraid we've got a breech presentation.'

'She's your patient. How are you going to handle the delivery? Are you going to do a Caesarian?'

Lucinda took a deep breath. 'I'm going to discuss it with the patient. I'll give her all the facts. I'm sure she'd prefer not to have a Caesarian, so I'll probably make a breech delivery.'

'Which is going to be very tricky,' he said, with ominous calm.

Lucinda faced Jonathan across the delivery table. He had made no reference to their disagreement of the previous evening during the few brief verbal exchanges that had been necessary that day. They were both on the same side now, fighting for the life of mother and baby.

The mother was now very distressed. As Lucinda had anticipated, she had asked not to have a Caesarian, but now she was literally begging for some more pethidine to ease the pain.

'Not at the moment, Kitty,' Lucinda said gently. 'I want you to co-operate for just a little while longer. I know you're exhausted, but we're nearly there. Breathe into the mask. . .'

The tiny buttocks of the foetus were pressed

against the perineum. Lucinda looked across at Jonathan. 'I'll have to do an episitomy,' she told him.

'Of course you will. Get on with it! I'll infiltrate the perineum with lignocaine.'

She looked down at Kitty Dawson, who was now past caring. Lucinda began to explain what she had to do, but the patient had stopped listening. Another one of her ideals about to be broken! Quickly Lucinda made a lateral incision in the perineum. Then she deftly eased out the foetus.

She could feel the general relief in the delivery-room when the baby gave its first cry.

Wrapping the tiny, slippery infant in a towel, she told the mother, 'You've got a little girl.'

With tears streaming down her cheeks, Kitty Dawson stretched out her arms.

Lucinda pushed open the door of the staff common-room. There was only one other person in the room.

Jonathan reached for the coffee percolator and poured out another cup. 'Here, drink this; you look all in.'

She ran a hand through her hair, conscious of the fact that she hadn't even combed it since delivering the Dawson baby. She took the coffee-cup he was holding out towards her. 'Thanks. I must confess I feel almost as exhausted as Kitty Dawson.'

'How is she?' he asked evenly.

'Still full of guilt because she hasn't got any breast milk yet. Sister Bradwell's giving the baby a bottle at the moment.'

'And I suppose she's full of guilt because she took painkillers and had a episiotomy.'

'Of course. When a birth doesn't go according to plan these idealistic mothers think it's all their fault.'

'I know,' he said quietly. 'Your friend Julia was just the same.'

'Julia?' Lucinda stared at him wide-eyed. 'But she told me you insisted she have a Caesarian. She said she'd pleaded with you to deliver the baby naturally, that there was absolutely no reason why it shouldn't have been.'

'It was a more difficult case than this one,' he said, in a low voice. 'A breech presentation, and the foetus showing signs of distress. Julia Lazelle had abandoned all idea of a natural birth by this time. She'd begged me for some more pethidine, and when I suggested a Caesarian she jumped at it.'

He paused, his dark eyes focused on Lucinda's face, watching her reaction carefully. 'It was only afterwards that she told me she felt guilty at giving in, as she called it. I told her she hadn't given in. She'd accepted that advances in surgery and technology must be used when appropriate. I think it was pride that made her invent the story she told you.'

Lucinda looked up into Jonathan's eyes, desperately searching for some indication that he still cared for her, in spite of everything. 'I'm sorry, Jonathan. I had no idea. . . I should have trusted you. I know we have our professional differences, but. . .'

'Look, we're both tired. Go and get some sleep. I

don't want to discuss it any more.' He stood up and moved towards the door.

'Jonathan!' she called.

He turned enquiringly in the open doorway.

'You were going to tell me some important news about. . .'

'Lucinda, I've had enough for one day!'

Lucinda hurried across the muddy path towards the Rathbone house. He needn't think she was going to wait any longer to hear the news about her father! If he'd wanted her to be patient, he shouldn't have hinted in the first place.

She stubbed her toe on an uneven stone in the path. Ouch! She slipped her foot out of her shoe and rubbed it. She would have to get some lights along this section of the path. . .that was if she stayed long enough to see the new scheme through! The way she was feeling at the moment, she had a good mind to hand in her notice. Jonathan Rathbone could keep his hospital and run it entirely as it pleased him. See if she cared!

There was a light shining on the porch. The door opened almost as soon as she touched the knocker.

'I knew you'd come!' Jonathan was standing in the doorway, the light from the hall shining on his dark, ruffled hair.

Lucinda thought she'd never seen him looking so maddeningly desirable and at the same time so infuriating. 'What made you think I'd come?' she asked defiantly.

He put out his hands and grasped hers, drawing

her into the warmth of the house. 'I know you can't resist a challenge. . .even though I wanted you to wait until tomorrow. I've been playing for time ever since my mother told me.'

'Told you what?' she asked breathlessly, aware that he was still holding both her hands.

He released one of her hands and pulled her against him, his arm around her shoulders. 'Come into the drawing-room,' he said.

She glanced at the grandfather clock, surprised to find it was almost midnight. Jonathan was busying himself trying to resurrect the fire in the hearth.

'I'm not cold,' she said hastily, longing for him to come back to her side.

He joined her on the sofa, placing an arm around her shoulders. 'It would have been better if you'd waited until tomorrow, because that's when he arrives.'

Her eyes widened. 'Not. . .not my father?'

He smiled happily. 'My mother's been trying to contact him since she found out who you were. She was the only person who knew who he was.' He paused. 'I've only just learned the whole story myself. Apparently your mother, Vanessa, was more like a daughter to my mother. When Vanessa died, my mother was heartbroken, and she decided she was never going to become so emotionally involved with a patient again.'

'But why was Vanessa so important to your mother?'

'Vanessa was actually born at the hospital soon after it was founded. As a child, she suffered from recurring bouts of severe bronchitis and spent long periods here during the winter. Her parents. . .' he smiled at Lucinda '. . .that's your grandparents, both died when Vanessa was in her early teens. My mother accepted her into a special unit for orphans in the hospital. And it was there that Vanessa met your father.'

Lucinda felt a shiver of excitement running down her spine. 'Was he an orphan too?'

Jonathan smiled. 'No. He was a young medical student. He was nineteen when he met the sixteen-year-old Vanessa. The falling in love was mutual, according to my mother. When Vanessa told her she was pregnant, my mother told her that she must tell the baby's father, but Vanessa begged my mother to keep his identity secret. She didn't want anyone to know, saying it would ruin his career to be saddled with a wife and child. She insisted that she could bring up the baby by herself. According to my mother Vanessa was a very strong-willed girl. . .like someone I know not a million miles from here!'

Lucinda looked up into his face, relieved to see that he was smiling. 'Go on,' she whispered hoarsely.

'So my mother was sworn to secrecy. Reluctantly, she joined in the conspiracy and told the boyfriend that Vanessa didn't want to see him any more. Somehow they managed to keep the pregnancy a secret from him. But after the baby. . .after you were born, Vanessa decided she wanted to see Richard again. . .'

'Richard,' Lucinda repeated softly. 'Is that my father's name?'

'Yes; Richard Warrender. . .but let me finish. My mother had told Vanessa to remain in bed after the birth but, being the stubborn, self-willed girl she was, she decided to take the matter into her own hands. One night, when you were just a few days old, she went out of the hospital, leaving you in the nursery with the other babies, being cared for by the night staff. No one knows exactly what happened, but it seemed as if Vanessa was trying to get across town to Richard's family home. She had no money with her, so she must have gone on foot. It was a freezing cold January night. The police found her in the early morning sheltering from the snow under Charing Cross Bridge, but by then her weak chest had been affected. She was brought back to the hospital and. . .'

And she died from pneumonia,' Lucinda finished in a quiet voice of acceptance. 'And Dr Mary didn't consider informing Richard Warrender about any of this?'

Jonathan shook his head. 'It had been Vanessa's initial wish that she shouldn't be allowed to disrupt his career, and my mother decided that Vanessa had been right. In the event, he went on to be very successful. He went out to the States soon after qualifying and he's a medical consultant now in New York. When I say now, I don't mean at this actual minute, because to my knowledge he's somewhere over the Atlantic. Would you like to come with me to Heathrow early in the morning?'

Would she! 'But why is he coming over?' she asked.

'I persuaded my mother to tell me everything she knew about your background. You see, I do have a vested interest. And when she admitted that she knew who your father was, I suggested it might be a good idea to put him in the picture. My mother gave me all the details and agreed that I could contact him. He was over the moon with the news that he has a daughter. You see, his wife was never able to have children.' He moved towards her, his arm tightening around her shoulder. 'Dr Warrender was also delighted to hear that I'm hoping to become his son-in-law.'

Lucinda pulled herself away, her pulses racing. 'You've got a nerve!' she exclaimed. 'What makes you think I'd even consider being friends with a self-opinionated man like you?'

She kept her eyes deliberately averted, knowing instinctively that it was impossible to disguise her happiness.

Jonathan gave a boyish laugh. 'If I can force myself to ignore your impossible ideals and agree to differ with you, then surely you can agree to compromise?'

She turned back to look at him and he caught her in his arms. 'You know, we make a great team really. And we don't spend all our time in the hospital, after all. You'll have to take some time off to have a family and. . .'

'Hey, steady on! You've got the cart before the

horse! Would you mind giving me a decent proposal? Something I can remember to tell the family about in years to come. . . Oh, Jonathan!' Suddenly she broke off, overwhelmed by the wonderful realisation that she was actually to have a real family at long last. . .her own natural family!

He pulled her against his chest, smothering her face with kisses. 'Darling, will you marry me?'

But her answer, when it came, was too muffled to be recognisable.

Life and death drama in this gripping new novel of passion and suspense

Following a vicious a tack on a tough proper developer and his beaut ful wife, eminent surgec David Compton fougl fiercely to save both live little knowing just ho deeply he would becom involved in a complex we of deadly revenge. Ginet Irving, the cool and pra tical theatre sister, was a enigma to David, b could he risk an affair wit the worrying threat to h career and now the sini ter attempts on his life?

WORLDWIDE

Price: £3.99 Published: May 1991

Available from Boots, Martins, John Menzies, W.H. Smith, Woolworths and other paperback stockists.

Also available from Mills and Boon Reader Service, P.O. Box 236, Thornton Road, Croydon, Surrey CR9 3RU

SPARKLING NEW TALENT

Every year we receive over 5,000 manuscripts at Mills & Boon, and from these a few names stand out as the fresh new talent for exciting romantic fiction.

Never before in paperback, we proudly present:

CHRISTINE GREIG
A Night-time Affair
JESSICA HART
A Sweet Prejudice
JOANNA NEIL
Wild Heart
CATHY WILLIAMS
A Powerful Attraction

reat yourself to a feast of love, rama and passion with the st romantic fiction from the st of Mills & Boon's new thors.

ice: £5.80
ublished: March 1991

ailable from Boots, Martins, John Menzies, W. H. Smith, Woolworths and other paperback stockists.
so available from Mills and Boon Reader Service, P.O. Box 236, Thornton Road, Croydon, Surrey, CR9 3RU.

Mills Boon